Trust me . . .

She swallowed, straightened her shoulders, and followed him into the darkness, guided only by the rustle and thud of his feet ahead of her. She knew she had placed a lot of trust, maybe even her life, in this man's hands . . .

Cobwebs brushed against her fingers. Dust floated in the air. How long since anyone had walked here? The thick ebony air began to make her feel trapped. The feeling of being smothered wrapped around her. She shivered, wishing she had worn her jacket.

Just as she thought she might start screaming, they stopped. She heard the click of a lock, the twist of a doorknob . . . and slowly the door opened.

THE DARK CHRONICLES

BOOK 2

The Gallery

BARBARA STEINER

AN AVON FLARE BOOK

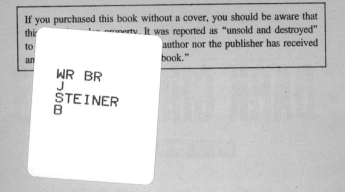
THE DARK CHRONICLES, BOOK 2: THE GALLERY is an original publication of Avon Books. This work has never before appeared in book form.

AVON BOOKS
A division of
The Hearst Corporation
1350 Avenue of the Americas
New York, New York 10019

Copyright © 1995 by Barbara Steiner
Published by arrangement with the author
Library of Congress Catalog Card Number: 94-96773
ISBN: 0-380-77689-8
RL: 6.6

First Avon Flare Printing: July 1995

AVON FLARE TRADEMARK REG. U.S. PAT. OFF. AND IN OTHER COUNTRIES, MARCA REGISTRADA, HECHO EN U.S.A.

Printed in the U.S.A.

RA   10   9   8   7   6   5   4   3   2   1

For Betty Forster and Alice Keefer, artists,
who bring a lot of light into my life

one

WE ALL BECOME blind at night. For some, night has been a frightening phenomenon since we were old enough to know that monsters slip out after dark. They live in our closets and under our beds and hide along the hall that leads to the bathroom.

For LaDonna Martindale the darkness was comforting. Darkness hid the squalid home where she never took friends. Darkness softened the tattered curtains and muted the water circles on the faded wallpaper in her room.

Neither her home nor her room was a place where LaDonna felt comfortable. Her mother had died when she was ten. She had always worked, so LaDonna learned household chores at an early age. Continuing them was easy, but she still missed her mother. They had been close, and her mother was in awe of LaDonna's talent. She was the one who always found money for paint, brushes, and canvas. "You must work at something you love, LaDonna. Never forget that." LaDonna repeated her mother's words to herself often.

Her father worked shifts, cleaning the buildings at the college, so she seldom saw him. His moods were unpredictable and LaDonna had learned long ago that avoiding him—not trying to guess what mood he was in—worked best for her.

The job she was offered toward the end of her senior year was perfect.

She was messing with a painting in the art room when Mr. Rodriguez, Roddy to his students, stopped and studied it for a few seconds.

"Awful, isn't it?" LaDonna said, wanting to cover her easel with her paint rag.

Roddy smiled and shrugged as if to say, it's not the end of the world. "It's not *that* bad. It's not that good either, not original enough. Anyone could have painted it."

"And I'm not just anyone." She said it before he could, not believing the words, even though he told her almost every day. The mantra kept her trying. *I'm not just anyone. I'm not just anyone. I'm special. One person thinks I'm special.*

"That's right. Now if you could just believe it." Roddy read her mind as he perched on the edge of a table. "Would you like an after school job, LaDonna?"

He caught her by surprise, but she didn't have to think it over long. "I—I sure would. I'm getting paint poor."

"Join the world of struggling artists. We buy paint before we buy food." Roddy didn't look like an artist. He wasn't thin with hollow cheeks. He had a round, Santa Claus face with brown eyes that squinted shut when he laughed. A silver Navajo belt buckle rode on his expansive stomach. But he dressed like an artist. His jeans had patches on the patches, his smock was paint smeared. His spattered tennis shoes had been cheap to start with, and the right one sported a hole where a toe poked up. She wondered if his wife, whom LaDonna thought incredibly beautiful, was ashamed to be seen with him.

Art class was last period, and Roddy seemed relaxed. But LaDonna knew he was eager to work on a mural the new rec center east of town had commissioned. Sometimes she stayed and painted for a couple of hours, too. She hadn't decided about today.

"A job would keep her off the streets." Johnny Blair overheard Roddy's question. He stepped over and tugged at LaDonna's single braid that hung halfway down her back. "Go for it, Martindale."

3

She made a face at Johnny and kept painting. "What would I be doing?" she asked Roddy.

"I have a good friend who runs the college's art gallery. Normally the job would go to a college student. And frankly, he's offered it to three people. One girl tried and quit after one hour on the job. None of them could work in the only room available in the art building—a basement room."

"That's curious," LaDonna said. "I wonder why not."

"Anyway, I've told Glen you'll be in his department next fall, so he'll bend some rules. They have a basement stacked with art left to them by estates—well-meaning alumni. Most of it has never been unpacked."

"And I'd unpack it," LaDonna caught on.

"Not just unpack it, but look it over, catalogue it, decide whether or not the work has any merit. If the gallery should keep it stored for rotating exhibitions, or dispose of it discreetly." Roddy smiled, probably anticipating LaDonna's next remark.

"They'd trust my judgement?"

"I assured Glen he could. I told him you were the most promising artist I've had in a long time."

4

"Uh-hum." Johnny cleared his throat loudly.

"Stick with your piano, Blair. Not everyone has multiple talents like I do." Roddy grinned at LaDonna. They both liked to tease Johnny, and he was sweet about taking it.

"And what are your other achievements, Rodriguez?" Johnny asked.

"I'm a great cook. Too good." Roddy pushed himself off the table and patted his round belly. "Both my wife and my doctor say twenty pounds have to go."

"You're the best teacher I've ever had," LaDonna added.

"I can't do any more for you, LaDonna. You have to take a leap of faith soon or give it up."

Mr. Rodriguez had never mentioned giving up to her before. Was he getting discouraged with her work? She had to admit that *she* was. Maybe a change of scenery, this job would help. If she saw enough bad work, she'd believe in herself again.

She decided quickly. She wanted this job, spooky basement or not. "What do I have to do to get the job, and when can I start?"

"Today if you like. Glen's there till five. Go up on the campus and talk to him. You pretty much have the job if you want it. He can tell you what he expects of you, and your hours—which I think are flexible."

"I'll walk with you," Johnny offered. "I have a piano lesson at four, and then I'll practice for a couple of hours."

If LaDonna had a friend, it was Johnny. They both fell into the dweeb category at Bellponte High. Dweeb, nerd—whatever you wanted to call someone who wasn't in the popular crowd, those who walked to their own drummers—the label fell into the social register just above punker, cowboy, or druggie. The artists, theater majors, and musicians were at least looked on as borderline dweebs, weird, but still not popular cheerleaders or worshipped athletes.

Friends were the least of LaDonna's worries. She liked being alone. She lived to paint. There wasn't much time left over for a social life.

She dipped her paint brush in a jar of dirty water behind her. "Okay, you're on, Johnny Blair. This wasn't going well anyway."

Johnny glanced at it and went back to his own easel. He was honest enough not to say, "Yes it was, it's wonderful."

"Maybe you need a change of scenery," he said. "School buildings are depressing." His crooked smile lit up a face that was even plainer than hers.

One of the world's thinnest people,

Johnny had a wry sense of humor usually ascribed to fat people. Everything was funny to him, and he had a repertoire of sick jokes that would fill an encyclopedia. If he wrote a book it would be called *The Complete Guide to Dark Humor*.

Bushy, corn silk-colored hair would never lie down. His horn-rimmed glasses were always slipping off. One or more zits exploded on his chin. But he had the most beautiful hands LaDonna had ever seen. Long, strong fingers, a pianist's fingers. If he wasn't at home at his own piano, he was at the college in a practice room. If anyone she knew succeeded in the arts, it would be Johnny. All he cared about was his music. And maybe, just a little, her. Not a romantic caring. But a human caring. They marched to a similar beat.

When the bell rang, they strolled, rather than marched, up the steep Seventeenth Street hill to the campus. Neither spoke. LaDonna took deep breaths of the reasonably clear air and marveled at the spring colors. Her paintings were usually darker, winter paintings she could call them. What if she tried a pink and lilac palette tomorrow? Would that be a leap of faith for her?

"This is my favorite time of year." Johnny finally spoke. "Everything is new, fresh. The smell is incredible." He breathed deeply.

"I didn't think you ever knew what season it was."

"I'm not a total recluse."

"You would be if you didn't come up here to practice," she teased, tossing a pine cone toward a searching squirrel.

"My parents can't afford a grand piano."

"And one would fill your entire living room."

Johnny lived close to the Martindales in a similar small frame house. "Isn't it amazing that two such talented people sprang from such a humble neighborhood?"

"Someday people will drive by your house and say 'Johnny Blair lived here. His first piano has been gold plated.'"

"Are you kidding? As soon as we leave those houses will be torn down to make room for more one-bedroom, ticky-tacky condos that rent for nine hundred dollars a month."

"I don't care. As long as our parents get rich from selling the land." Johnny's mother worked so hard, it was great to think of her retiring rich. LaDonna's father probably worked hard, too—if anyone was watching him. At home he was a couch potato.

Bellponte College had a beautiful campus. Scores of old trees lined the sidewalks and shaded grass that was fast

8

becoming spring green. Sprinklers turned on and off automatically even though they'd had several good rains. A few students strolled or sprawled on benches visiting or studying, but most had finished classes for the day.

The art gallery was in one of the oldest buildings on the hill, square, covered with vines of woodbine. All the original college buildings were constructed from wine-colored brick with dark green wood trim. All had off white-tiled roofs.

"Break a leg." Johnny grinned and turned right toward Old Main.

The large building once housed the entire college. Now it loomed over the north campus like two Victorian ladies in tight corsets, reining over a central drawing room. Twin towers, each with a twisting, winding staircase, housed many small, soundproof practice rooms. In between, an auditorium was the site of concerts, plays, and special events.

Johnny had a regularly scheduled time for one room with a piano. Often he would drop by and hunt another that was vacant.

LaDonna waved and hurried toward the art building. There she learned Glen Walker was expecting her. Roddy must have called after she left. A secretary directed her down the squeaky hall to a musty room. All the rooms in the building probably smelled this way because of age. No amount of fresh air through open windows could blow out that hint of time.

"Miss Martindale." Glen Walker smiled and reached for her hand. "I expected someone with a New York success look after that build-up from Roddy."

LaDonna liked him immediately. "Sorry. This is my struggling student image. Less intimidating. I wanted you to know I needed the job."

"Roddy will have one of my ears if I don't give it to you. But I think I should tell you, I offered it to several of my students already. They all said they didn't think they could work here in the basement."

LaDonna noticed he didn't mention the girl who worked for an hour and quit. "Let me guess. The basement is dark and gloomy and smells of hundred-year-old dust." LaDonna smiled at Glen Walker.

"Right on. Not to mention that this whole building is full of spooks. Let's go down there. I'll show you before you commit yourself." He led the way down the hall, then opened a door onto a narrow staircase.

LaDonna did feel as if she was going into some underground vault, each squeak of the stairs saying, *Go back, go back while there's time*. She laughed at her runaway imagination.

There was one wall switch at the bottom of the stairs. The rest of the overhead hall lights had strings to pull them on.

"The glamorous nineteenth century." Walker took them from string to string, fumbling for the last while LaDonna waited in dim light in the doorway. A hollow room was piled with boxes. A large wooden table stood in the middle of the room. Bare cement walls had only cobwebs and cracks running ceiling to floor for decor. "The room is cold, even in summer."

LaDonna glanced around, then peeked into one box that had been slit open. She pulled out a sketch and laid it on the table. It was of the misty, softly-rounded mountains that marked the western boundary of the city. Glen Walker studied it with her.

"People have always been fascinated by Bellponte, the river, the hills, the old architecture. This isn't bad, but I'd guess it's a study for a painting," Walker said as she started to reach back into the box. "So you think you can work in this space?" He stopped her. "You won't be afraid down here alone, will you?"

"Of course not. Roddy said I could set my own hours. Can I work at night?"

Walker stared at her before he spoke, his dark eyes serious. "I'll give you a key.

You can work anytime you like. But you won't stay too late, will you? I'll worry."

"I like the night, Mr. Walker. The darkness will soften this old building."

He kept looking at her for a few seconds. "Okay. I'm glad. I don't have time to sort these paintings myself. And the job needs to be done. We got a small grant for your pay. When that runs out, I'll find more." He started back across the basement, expecting her to follow.

She did. But not until she'd stood still for a moment longer. A cloud of air swirled around her. She lifted her hand, palm up, as if testing for moisture from a cloudy sky. Something brushed her fingers, velvet-soft, kitten-warm, alive.

"What is it?" Walker asked softly.

"Oh, nothing," LaDonna said quickly. "I was just curious. It's nothing." She followed him, pulling off the light in the room, letting her fingers linger on the beaded metal chain and the dirty string.

There was a presence in the empty room. She couldn't explain it. But she knew it was there. And she knew it welcomed her. For one moment, she was startled, but she didn't feel the least bit frightened. She didn't think she ever would.

This was the perfect job for her. It was as if—as if he—as if the job—had been waiting for her to come along.

two

LADONNA WAITED UNTIL the next morning to tell her dad. "Yesterday I got an after school job. Mr. Rodriguez helped me get it. I'll work at the art gallery on campus."

Her father looked at LaDonna as if surprised someone had spoken at breakfast. He was on a day shift this week and had probably stayed up too late watching television. He struggled to wake up. On weekends or when he worked nights, he slept late, went to football games, basketball games, or baseball games—whatever sport was in season. LaDonna seldom saw him, but that suited her fine.

She usually came in after school, took a plate of food and a glass of milk to her room to study or paint and sketch. She found most of television programming dumb. If she read, the book was for a class. She and Johnny sometimes went to a movie on the weekend. Otherwise her life was pretty much solitary and one-sided.

"Do you think we're normal?" she had once said to Johnny. "Of course not," was his reply. "Who wants to be normal?"

"How much are you getting paid?" Mr. Martindale asked, laying down his newspaper for a few seconds.

"I—I forgot to ask." LaDonna realized she didn't care. "Minimum wage, I guess."

"You won't be coming home at night, will you, LaDonna?" Her father sipped his coffee. "That campus isn't safe after dark."

"I can set my own hours. I might work some at night. I'm not afraid."

"Sometimes it's smart to be afraid."

"I'm careful, Dad. I'll be fine. You don't need to worry." It surprised LaDonna that her father even cared. He was in his mellow mood today.

"I know you can take care of yourself, honey," he said. "I'm glad you got a job." He went back to studying the newspaper.

End of conversation.

LaDonna had taken care of herself since she was ten. She didn't mind being on her own.

Nothing mattered to LaDonna except

painting. When her work was going well, she was happy. When work was going wrong, nothing seemed right. Her last three paintings were amateurish, disappointing. She couldn't transfer what she had in her mind onto the canvas. She had dumped them into the trash bin at school. LaDonna would do anything to get back on track.

"How was breakfast at LaDonna's?" Johnny asked, grinning.

It was great to see that lopsided smile every morning. LaDonna realized how she depended on it. What would she do without Johnny?

"Scintillating." LaDonna grimaced and set a leisurely pace for walking up the hill to school.

"Oh, big word. Someone must have spoken today."

"I had to speak first." She had told Johnny about her home life a long time ago. The explanation had taken about three minutes. "I told Dad I got a job."

"So you took it. You work. I'll practice. We can walk home together. The campus—"

LaDonna put out her hand like a traffic cop. "If one more person worries about me this week, I'm going to feel special, Johnny, like Roddy keeps telling me. Just want to warn you." LaDonna felt warm inside to think Johnny cared.

In an unexpected move, Johnny spun her around and hugged her. "You are special, Miss Nightingale."

Johnny hadn't called her that since they were in grade school. She thought he'd forgotten. When they first met in third grade he'd said, "Nightingale?" LaDonna remembered giggling and saying, "No, Martindale, silly." But for a long time he'd called her Lady LaDonna Nightingale. And sometimes he played the Beatles's song called "Lady Madonna"—only he misquoted saying Lady LaDonna—for her on his piano, making his living room sound like a honky-tonk. The first couple of times his mother came into the room, wondering at the noise and giggling. Then she got used to it being them, acting silly.

The hug felt good. Neither said anything for a couple of blocks. LaDonna wondered if they were getting to be more than friends. A part of her wished they would. A part said, no, friends is best. A part of her said, you're silly to even think about it. Johnny is your best friend—your only friend.

Luis Rodriquez was her friend, she realized. As much as a teacher can be a friend. This was her third year in one of his art classes.

Whoopee-do, she thought. The girl with

16

two friends. She felt her mouth stretch into a big grin.

"Penny?" Johnny offered.

"I'm glad you're my friend, Johnny Blair. Thanks."

"No problem, ma'am." He lifted an imaginary hat. "Glad to be of service."

"Are we weird, Johnny? Should I give it all up and go out for the cheerleading squad?"

"Think you'd make it?" Johnny fingered the piece of tissue on his chin. Zit or razor cut? she wondered. Shaving was making his skin clear up. When had he started to be cute?

"No. But I don't think I'm going to make Miss-Likely-to-Succeed, either."

"You've been in a slump before. I think it's nothing that a double chocolate mocha almond fudge at Josh and John's after school wouldn't cure."

"You think it's that simple?" LaDonna laughed. At least Johnny was cheering her up. "I'm willing to try anything."

"Yes. Deal?" Johnny put out the palm of his hand.

LaDonna slapped it. "Deal. On our way to the campus after art class."

By the time art class was over, LaDonna needed chocolate. A student teacher showed up in their art class. Roddy had accepted student teachers before, but never one as nerdy as Eric Hunter. He was a hunter all right—a predator. He had his arm around every female in class before the hour was over—when Roddy wasn't looking. And LaDonna could see that Marilee Morris, of course, was already in love with Eric by the end of the period. Marilee fell in and out of love so fast, you'd get dizzy trying to keep up with her social life.

LaDonna spun around to face Eric before he could touch her.

Eric grinned at her, probably because she had anticipated his move. "Rodriquez says you're the most promising artist in the class. Got a portfolio I can look at?" He made the word sound suggestive.

"No. I've thrown out my last three attempts."

"Oh, a perfectionist."

"A realist."

A small smile flitted across Eric's lips and his dark eyes undressed her. His eyes were nearly black and could have been beautiful. He was clearly a weight lifter, looking more like an artist's model than an artist. More like a jock than a painter. Tall, compact, Eric held himself loosely, draping one arm around the class skeleton to talk to her. A square jaw brought to mind a picture of a halfway civilized cave man. Put him in a leopard skin and maybe he'd be successful at painting cave walls.

"Smile at him and he'll drag you away by your braid," Johnny whispered behind her as Eric gave up and sauntered away, looking for easier prey.

"Doesn't he wish?" LaDonna didn't even bother to whisper. But she laughed inside to know how much she and Johnny thought alike.

"I'm glad you still have good taste in men." Johnny wiped his paint brush on a muddy rag. "Ready for a taste adventure in chocolate?"

"Please." She tossed her brush into a mayonnaise jar of water and wiped her hands on her smock. Catching Roddy's eye, she waved, grabbed her notebook and geometry text, and headed for the back door. "Ah, fresh air."

"It's going to be a long semester," Johnny agreed, knowing she meant their enduring Eric Hunter.

"Why us? I lived for sixth period."

"Maybe he'll cool off. Or maybe Merilee Morris will take the bait. He'd be an improvement over Leo the Linebacker."

"Why, Johnny Blair. You do keep up with the Bellponte High soaps."

"Gives me something to do in chemistry class."

They climbed Seventeenth Street hill, then cut across the college campus to The

Hill shops. Josh and John's was half way up Thirteenth Street and packed with hungry students. An outside table freed up just as they got there.

"Grab that table, LaDonna," Johnny said. "I'll treat."

LaDonna was glad to sit there and watch the ant hill of students coming and going. She resolved to speak to Roddy before she'd let Eric spoil art class. Then she put him aside to think about her first day on her new job and the sinful ice cream cone Johnny was bringing her.

"I'll be sick," she joked.

"But think how sensuous it'll be going down." Johnny groaned with pleasure, licking chocolate drips from his fingers.

"Sensuous? Are you going through puberty again, Blair?"

"God, I hope not. I'd break my fingers first."

LaDonna looked at the long, strong fingers wrapped around the cone. Brown milky rivers oozed over the side of the double dip and down his knuckles. She shivered, and not from the cold ice cream.

Talk about puberty, I am going nuts, she thought. What's wrong with me? When did I stop thinking of Johnny Blair as more than a brother?

"What time are you going home?" Johnny asked when they headed back towards the campus.

"Oh, don't make me say, Johnny. I need to lose myself for a few hours."

"Ditto. I'll see you if I see you."

"Thanks, Johnny. For the ice cream *and* for understanding."

LaDonna practically ran to the art building, tugged open the heavy door, and stepped into the hall.

She found the small door at the end of the hall that looked like a closet, pulled it closed behind her after flipping on the dim light over the stairs.

She took a deep breath before she stepped down. The word "cave" flashed back into her mind. How silly.

She bounced lightly down the steps, hearing them creak underfoot, snapped off the two-way light at the bottom, then went from string to string lighting the way to the room where she'd work.

The air seemed thick with a century's collection of dust. Her feet padded in slow motion across wine-painted cement which had faded and mottled to several shades of pink and purple as well as the deep shade of vintage brew. The arm that reached for the next string felt heavy, rose slowly.

When she reached her workroom, she felt guilty not turning off the lights behind her, although she would have liked to keep them all on, so she went back. As she started at the bottom of the stairs again, pulling the lights off, darkness followed her. But the lighted room pulled her along, like sun sliding out from clouds after a rain. Something inside her yearned for the light. She moved faster and faster until when she stepped back into the lighted room, she was out of breath.

"You're being silly," she whispered. "You'll talk yourself out of this job like the last girl to try it."

She leaned on the table in the middle of the floor and looked around. There was a closed door at the far end. One chair. Otherwise the room was bare. As empty as a room could get. The longer she stood and looked around, though, the better she felt.

The hall had frightened her. Not the room. She relaxed. Breathed normally. The room was safe. She closed the door to the hall. Closed herself in.

She piled her books on the only chair, wooden, hard, straight backed. Quickly she lifted a painting from its box. Placed it on the table. Studied it.

Greens and blues blurred. A brown cottage wavered as if under water. She blinked her eyes. Blinked again. Looked behind her. Looked at both closed doors.

She concentrated on the painting again. Sun slid out from under clouds like the room, when it was lighted. Warm. The sun warmed the painting. The room was warm, not too warm. Comfortable. She would have expected it to be cool. The air in the room surrounded her like—like Johnny's arms. His hug this morning. The room was a warm presence.

No. Not the room. Something. Someone. The same someone she had sensed the first time she was here.

She—she was not alone.

three

"WHO'S THERE?" HER voice echoed in the hollow room, resonated in her mind.

There, there, there. Here, here, here.

She felt foolish asking. No one was here with her.

She laughed. Pulled another painting from the carton.

She had worked in the art building feeling comfortable with whoever or whatever was there with her—no longer questioning it—for three weeks when the first painting appeared, hanging on the wall.

In that three weeks, twenty-one days, five hundred and four hours, thirty-thousand two hundred and forty minutes—she'd worked out this triviality one day in algebra class—she felt she was running through molasses. Every day moved in slow motion. She swam underwater, treading minutes and hours uselessly.

Her art work got worse. During the class hour, she stared at an empty canvas, or one muddied with paint-overs.

"I've seen slumps, LaDonna. I've been blocked," Roddy said, looking over her shoulder. "This is classic."

"What can I do?" LaDonna asked. She begged Roddy to help her, pleaded silently for someone, something to happen.

"I don't know," Roddy admitted. "Is anything wrong at home?"

"No." Her home life was out of the ordinary, but it had been that way for so long she was used to it. She ignored her father. She lived for art class and the time she spent painting in her room.

The student teacher, Eric Hunter, tried to put the moves on her again. She hardly noticed. He gave up and looked for easier prey, but often she caught him looking at her.

"What's wrong with you, LaDonna?" Johnny asked on the way up to the campus. "You're not here. Correct me if I'm wrong, but you left three weeks ago. When you got that job. Are you all right? Is the job all right?"

Should she try to explain to Johnny? What—explain what? That she now lived for that job. That she felt alive only when she was in that basement room, closed in with—with—with whatever, whoever was there. He'd think she was nuts.

She thought she was nuts.

As she approached the art building she began to feel as if she was surrounded by some field of energy. Her mind seemed to vibrate. Prickles of excitement ran up and down her spine. The hair on the back of her neck rose and sent shivers through her body.

"I'll try to explain it soon, Johnny. Something is going on and I don't know what. I don't know *how* to tell you about it. But I've got to tell someone. And soon."

Johnny didn't press her to explain. But he did pick up on her apprehension, her confusion. When they reached the art building, he turned and pulled her into his arms. Held her close for a minute or more. She snuggled into his shoulder, smelling his familiar scent, perspiration mixed with some spicy aftershave he'd probably stolen from his father. She couldn't imagine his buying it for himself. She wished he would stay with her. Even wished she'd never heard of this job.

Did she really?

"I'll come by your house tonight, LaDonna."

"No, don't. Please don't. I'll come to

26

your place. Is that all right? After dinner. About seven?"

"Please, LaDonna. I don't want to worry about you. But I am worried. You might as well know it."

"Thanks, Johnny." LaDonna stared into his blue eyes. "You're a good friend, Johnny Blair. The only one I have."

She pulled away and opened the art building's heavy door. The metal bar was cold on her hand. The lie was cold on her tongue. She had three friends. Johnny. Roddy.

And *him*.

The walk to the basement had become routine. Her feelings were anything but normal. There was a pull, like a room full of warm magnets, to the soft yellow light. She no longer needed to turn on each light on the way. She left the stair light on, followed the river of vibrating air to her space, tugged on the overhead chain. The warm air bathed her in well being, comforted her, transformed her beyond the warmth of Johnny's arms.

One night, at home alone, the word ghost floated into her mind. But ghosts were scary. And they drifted on cold currents, drafty swirls of energy. Besides, if her friend was a ghost, he meant no harm. He was not there to frighten her.

The bare concrete walls of the basement room depressed her. It didn't take long for her to do something about that. Around the top of each wall, about two feet down, ran a wooden railing from which to hang pictures. She didn't question why it was there. She didn't remember seeing it the first time she came here. Perhaps the room had not always been bare.

Carefully, she had weeded out the worst paintings, sketches, and placed them in a pile to be discarded. When she came across a good picture, or one that she wasn't sure about, she hung it. Soon she had created her own personal art gallery.

The paintings had done wonders for the bare room. Now it vibrated with color—well, not too much color. Most of the paintings were landscapes, all green and brown with some flowers and flowering trees. A few had water, so splashes of blue drew her eye and relieved the lush vegetation. A few of the paintings were impressionistic, but most were realistic, imitating photographs.

On one wall she had hung all the pictures of Bellponte, New York, or the Atlantic Ocean. A few were of the buildings on the college campus with their white tile roofs. Snowy landscapes and sailing scenes. Fall colors, New York's woods in golden red and orange flames, shimmering on sunny autumn days. Those colors were her favorites. She had hated the pink painting she'd tried to do.

Tonight as she turned, reviewing what she had selected so far as possible "keepers," she stopped.

On the south wall, at eye level, so she couldn't possibly miss it, hung another painting. One she hadn't placed there. One that was so different in style she would have noticed it immediately even had she tugged it from a cardboard carton.

She gasped at its haunting beauty. A shiver ran the full length of her body, leaving her limp. Stepping back, she leaned on the wooden table, grasping the edge with both hands.

For a fleeting moment she felt as if she had been sucked into the center of the landscape. Into the empty space that seemed to be waiting, waiting for her presence. Yet when she was there, in the picture, she felt a chill, an icy draft that left her frozen and breathless.

It took all her strength to return to the room. She blinked her eyes. Blinked again. She gained the distance she needed to be herself. To look at the picture, to study it without emotion.

The sky had the stormy brooding nature of an El Greco—that combination of light and dark the Italians called *chiaroscuro*. Blues, grays, black and white. At any moment lightning would splinter the clouds.

On either side, as if lining a street, waiting, stood many hooded figures, their gowns drawn with loose, sweeping brush strokes. Their eyes had the dark brooding stare favored by the Mexican painter José Orozco.

The center of the painting obsessed LaDonna, forced her to clutch the table as if it waited for her to come in. On the horizon floated the warm yellow light, the light she was drawn to every day when she came to work. Except in the painting, centered there, alone, the effect was one of loneliness, a haunting emptiness. A need. As if the artist was able to paint, by not painting, his yearning for something, someone. His hollow longing.

Suddenly LaDonna felt she couldn't breathe. She was suffocating. All the oxygen in the room was used up. Choking, she turned, twisted the slick door knob to escape, dashed down the hall, up the stairs, outside. Leaning on the cold bricks, she sucked in the cool, spring air. She breathed deeply until she felt normal, until her lungs could rise and fall in a normal rhythm.

Glen Walker stepped out of the art building while she fought for control. "LaDonna, how's it going? Sorry I haven't been down to check on you, but this se-

mester has been a scramble to keep up."
He didn't notice her distressed state. La-
Donna was grateful for that.

"You haven't been downstairs, Mr.
Walker? I've hung up some of the art. You
didn't come in and hang another painting
alongside those I've picked out?"

She knew he hadn't.

"No. I just don't have much free time.
I trust your judgement, LaDonna. Roddy
told me I could. And to tell the truth, I
don't expect you to find any masterpieces
in all that mess."

"Well—well—let's hope we're both surprised." She gave him permission to
leave. To hurry on his way. He was obviously pressed for time. She had regained
her composure.

"Sure. Goodnight. Don't work too late,
you hear?" He turned and walked briskly
toward the parking lot.

She could go back inside now. She had
been silly. She had let her imagination run
away, double time. A smile crept across
her face. What would *he* think of her?

She entered the building slowly. On
seeing that Walker's secretary, Mrs.
Coombs, was in her office, LaDonna had
an idea. She didn't know why she hadn't
thought of it before.

"Mrs. Coombs," she said, after waiting
for the secretary to get off the phone. "Do
you have the phone number of that girl

who tried to do this job that I'm doing? You know, the one who worked for an hour and quit."

Mrs. Coombs looked at LaDonna for a moment as if she had to remember what LaDonna meant. She didn't have to remember. "Mr. Walker told you that story after all? He said maybe he'd better keep it to himself and I agreed." She finally smiled.

"No, he didn't tell me. My art teacher at school mentioned it before I even came up here. I'm glad she didn't like working here, though. Her turning the job down was my good luck."

Mrs. Coombs had been looking back in her day timer while they talked. She took a sheet of scrap paper and scribbled on it. "Minette Waterson. Here's her number. Why do you want it? Anything wrong?" She asked the question as if she expected there to be a problem.

"No, nothing wrong. Curiosity, I guess. Thanks, Mrs. Coombs." LaDonna escaped before the secretary could question her further.

Well, almost. "LaDonna." Mrs. Coombs called her back. "You aren't working late at night any more, are you?"

"Not much. And I'm really careful. Don't worry about me."

"I do." Darlene Coombs looked like the

perfect grandmother. She probably worried about everyone.

LaDonna ran back downstairs, clutching the scrap of paper in her fist.

He wasn't there. The painting still hung on the wall. She hadn't imagined it. But he was gone. Usually he didn't leave until she left, or just before she felt exhausted, as if he knew she was going home. She was surprised to feel disappointed.

She reached for her notebook, tore out a sheet of paper, dug in her purse for a pen. What could she say? Anything she thought of sounded dumb. But, she had to say something.

This is hauntingly beautiful. I can't express my feelings about it. But you know, don't you? It touched me. It frightened me. I think its one of the best works of art I've ever seen. Would you share some others?

She taped the note on the gray, weathered frame. The wood looked as if it had been taken from an old building. The frame suited the picture perfectly.

LaDonna gathered her books, leaned on the table for another minute and studied the painting. She left early. It would be some kind of sacrilege to unpack any more of the mediocre paintings in the boxes stored around the room today.

She'd go find Johnny. He'd still be in the practice room. She wouldn't wait until after dinner. To her surprise, she'd only been in the basement an hour. Time didn't matter. She'd worked a lot of hours. Maybe too many. The grant money would run out too fast. If Mr. Walker didn't find more, the job would be over. She couldn't stand for this job to be over. She'd start working as many hours as she liked, but report only a few.

The idea of not returning to him was one she couldn't bear.

"I'll be back tomorrow," she whispered. "I can't stay any longer tonight. You understand, don't you?" She paused, but got no answer. "I know you do."

Snapping off the light, she walked slowly away from the painting with its haunting eyes and its lonely yearning.

four

THE NIGHT AIR caressed her cheeks, cooled them, cooled her body. She hadn't realized how warm she was. Her body was damp with perspiration. Soon she felt chilled. She walked faster.

A silver crescent of moon sailed across the eastern sky. The campus seemed empty and darker than usual. But the darkness felt like a velvet cloak, wrapping her in anonymity. She was no one, going nowhere. No one expected anything from her. The role suited her for a few minutes.

Varsity Pond glistened from the reflection of lights on wrought iron posts. She stopped at the bridge, leaned over, took a deep breath of the fresh wind, the shift from winter sleep to spring's awakening.

A noise in the shadows startled her.

Probably a couple making out, she thought, yet the rustle had spoiled her feeling of being alone. She walked slowly on, down the narrow alley behind two of the campus buildings.

Another shuffling sound caused her to look back, to feel someone was behind her, even following her. That was non-sense. She was spooked because of what had happened in the basement room. Now her imagination was going to dash away with her.

Nonetheless, she quickened her pace towards Old Main. The woods to her left were thick and dark. Lights lined the alley. More lights illuminated the street a couple of hundred yards below. But there was a band of shadowy pines and grassy lawn in between.

She was not a runner, but she picked up her pace so that her feet thudded in an almost-jog. She hated the apprehension that flooded over her, started a prickly feeling in her stomach. She had never been afraid anyplace at night. Why was she scaring herself now?

Old Main loomed ahead, looking as if it belonged in a gothic novel. She hurried onto the concrete porch, glanced back. No one was behind her, of course. No one had been in the woods, near the pond. Deer roamed all over west and central Bellponte. There were rabbits on campus as well as raccoons, squirrels—all sorts of little creatures that skitter or meander through the night woods.

The foyer of Old Main was barn-like. Ceilings high overhead were plastered in ornate designs favored at the turn of the century. LaDonna thudded up the first flight of steep stairs. The wooden floor and now wooden steps to the second floor creaked and groaned. Maybe she should have just gone home. Johnny wasn't going to like being interrupted.

By the time she reached the twisting stairs to the third floor, she had a lonely feeling of being the only one alive on the campus. It seemed strange, unnatural, not to have run into even one student.

Half running, she searched the brass numbers overhead until she located 339, Johnny's usual room. Grasping the knob and turning, she tumbled in as soon as the door opened.

A look of astonishment flitted across Johnny's face as his hands froze in mid-air over ivory keys. Bass notes trembled long after being struck. LaDonna bent across the curve of the baby grand and gasped, sucking in the musty air of the closet-like room.

"LaDonna? What's wrong? Are you all right?" Johnny came to life, stood, stepped around the piano and put his hand on her shoulder.

"I'm fine, Johnny, fine. I—I—just—lost it out there, spooked myself good. Why isn't there anyone on campus? Where is everyone tonight?"

"I'm right here." He grinned. "Who else were you looking for?" Johnny stepped back and studied her.

"You aren't mad, are you? I'm sorry to interrupt your practice. I needed—I needed—"

"Me? I'd like that." His blue eyes sparkled. Long, slim fingers rested on the shiny black wood. LaDonna averted her eyes to his hands, not able to keep looking into his eyes.

"Well, if it won't make you conceited, I guess so. I needed someone, and you were the closest one I knew of."

"Now you're trying to wiggle out of wanting to see *me*, not just anyone, but old Johnny Blair, counselor to artists, especially those of the female gender, smelling of oil paint."

In an uncharacteristic move, she reached up to him, hugged him tight. He hugged back, his flesh warm and comforting.

"Can you stop early, Johnny? I'll even buy pizza."

"You *are* desperate."

"Don't expect me to be this generous all the time." She turned, taking a deep

38

breath, collecting her composure. "This is an occasion."

"I'll stop. I'll stop. Or I'll come back later. I never could resist a damsel in distress."

"Okay, create a melodrama if you must, JB. Let's go. All of a sudden, I'm starving."

"When did you last eat?"

"I don't remember. It didn't seem important."

"That's your problem. Your blood sugar has dropped so low, you're hallucinating."

Johnny laughed, followed her out the door, locked it behind them. A tall, model-slim girl greeted them—him. "Hi, Johnny. Quitting early?"

"Pizza break. I shall return."

They both laughed as the girl stopped at a practice room two doors down. La-Donna found she wasn't breathing. For some reason she pictured the girl's long slim fingers on Johnny's arm. Johnny's hand smoothing down her wild, dark-red hair.

"*Now* I see another human being." La-Donna needed to comment on the girl's appearance. "Good friend?"

"You care?"

"Of course not. I—" LaDonna stammered, felt her face heat up, her cheeks redden.

Johnny laughed. "It's all right to be jealous. I don't mind. I guess I see almost as much of Katherine as I do you. She's just another musical genius."

Outside the building, people swarmed as if a class had just been dismissed. Couples, hand in hand, strolled towards the darkened pond. A cluster of students argued over some point as if continuing a class discussion. LaDonna looked around, thinking she had crossed from the art building in some kind of time warp. This scene was normal.

Teresa's had a twenty minute wait, making LaDonna even more hungry. Spicy tomato and pepperoni smells floated out to them while they sat on a bench in front of the restaurant.

"Want to talk or wait till you've eaten?"

"There's someone in the art building basement with me, Johnny." LaDonna blurted out her suspicion.

"Someone? Who?"

"I don't know. I haven't seen him. But I feel his presence. And tonight he'd left me a painting to look at."

"What kind of painting? Whose? Was it pornographic?"

"Of course not, Johnny. Don't tease me. I'm serious. I assume it was his painting. Why would he show me work from another artist?"

"Let me run this by again. Some guy is

pestering you at work, and tonight he asked you to look at one of his paintings?"

"You make it sound so ordinary, Johnny. It's not. I haven't seen this person. I think it's a man. I feel that he's there with me. He's been there from the very beginning. And when I came in this afternoon, a very different painting hung on the wall where I've been hanging those I've unpacked."

Johnny cleared his throat and frowned. One hand played with the braid on LaDonna's shoulder. LaDonna wished he'd stop. She didn't want to be distracted, but since he was probably unaware of what he was doing, she didn't speak.

"What kind of painting?" he asked again.

LaDonna pictured the scene in her mind again, thought about how to describe it. "Disturbing. Fairly dark colors. Monks or people in robes lining a street, as if—as if they were waiting for someone. Troubled sky. The center of the painting is lonely."

"The sky is troubled. The center is lonely. Sure this is a painting you're describing, LaDonna? You've been alone too much. You probably came and got me just in time."

"Yes, and I should have known you'd laugh at me." She breathed deeply, wishing she could just laugh about all of this.

"Hey, I'm not laughing. Look at my face. Is this laughter you see?" Johnny framed his face with both hands and widened his eyes. He needed a haircut badly. She thought of the scarecrow in *The Wizard of Oz*, his straw hair sticking up all whichaways.

She laughed, relaxing. "I guess I do sound nutty, but who left a painting, a good painting, hanging down there for me to see?"

"A struggling artist who'd do anything to get attention?"

"My attention? What could I do for him?"

"Who else's attention would he get if you're the only one working down there?"

"And I am."

"Let's go back to this feeling you've come up with." Johnny made a steeple with both hands, pressing his fingers together as if stretching them. "Do you believe in ghosts?"

LaDonna sat quietly herself for a few seconds. "I never have before now. Do ghosts paint?"

"Is the person who left the painting the same one who's—who's been haunting you?"

"Yes." She didn't even hesitate before she answered that question. She knew *he*'d hung the painting on the wall.

"Obviously this ghost paints then. Tell Walker your story." Johnny glanced at the door of the restaurant to see if anyone was looking for them to tell them a table was free. LaDonna felt he was more interested in eating than hearing her crazy story.

"I—I don't want to. He might make me stop working there."

"You want to stop?"

"No, I can't."

"You can't? You mean you need the money."

That wasn't what LaDonna meant at all. She lied. "Yes, paint is so expensive. I can't keep asking my dad for so much."

"Are you scared down there?"

"No, not really. I got a bit spooked tonight for some reason. Suddenly, the whole idea just seemed so strange."

"Yes, I'll agree with that. But *you* are strange, LaDonna Martindale." Johnny returned to his teasing. He squeezed LaDonna's shoulder.

"Someone followed me across the campus." She didn't mean to say that. The idea blurted out.

"This ghost followed you. I thought ghosts were supposed to stay in one place. One house per ghost. No moving around. Something happened in the art building to make him unhappy, so he's supposed to hang around there until he resolves it. Those are the ghost rules."

"How do you know so much about ghost behavior?"

"I see movies. Watch TV. Read. I'm fairly normal despite my obsession with my piano. You really think he followed you?"

"No. But someone did." Somehow she was sure of that.

"Blair." An outside speaker announced that their table was ready. Both of them stood slowly and moved towards the door.

"Let's eat. I'll walk you home. Will that make you feel better?" Johnny took her arm and steered her into a booth.

"Much better. Tomorrow I'll be back to normal, I promise, JB." She felt better being with Johnny. She hoped tomorrow the world would return to normal.

"No more 'Twilight Zone'?" Johnny hummed the music to the old TV show.

She smiled and shook her head, slid into a booth, and concentrated on the menu.

"Share your booth and I'll treat," said a voice behind LaDonna. She didn't have to turn around to know the speaker was Eric Hunter. And too much lilac perfume probably meant—LaDonna turned around to be sure—Merilee Morris. She was right. Wasn't this against some kind of unwritten rule? No teachers dating students. Hunter was a student teacher, but he was probably supposed to behave like faculty at Bellponte High while he was there.

Johnny looked at LaDonna as if to say, do we have to? But he moved over to let Eric slide in beside him. Instead Eric Hunter slid in beside LaDonna, close, too close. And Merilee sat beside Johnny and grasped his arm. She giggled and whispered in his ear. LaDonna hardly ever saw Johnny blush, but his face got pink and his lips formed a sheepish grin.

LaDonna suddenly lost her appetite. She scooted closer to the wall and studied her menu again. This was going to make the weird state of mind she'd gotten into this evening vanish.

five

JOHNNY BLAIR WAS often brutally honest. "I didn't think teachers were supposed to date students, Hunter."

"This is not a date, Blair. Don't panic. I ran into Merilee on the campus and found she hadn't eaten dinner. So why should two lonely people eat alone?"

Merilee giggled. "Yeah, why?" She blinked blue eyes at Johnny.

In her lap, LaDonna felt both hands tighten into fists. She took them out and flattened them on the table cloth.

"The hands of an artist," Eric Hunter commented, running one finger from the tip of LaDonna's middle finger to her wrist. She took her hands back and hid them in her lap again. She had stubby fingers, permanently paint stained unless she scrubbed with turpentine. But she'd never cared how her hands looked before.

She stared at her watch. "Oh, my gosh, Johnny. I completely forgot I told my dad I'd go to the basketball game with him tonight. We were supposed to pick up something to eat on the way. He's going to kill me." LaDonna jumped halfway to her feet and would have slid past Eric Hunter if he hadn't gotten the idea that she wanted him to move.

"I'll go with you," Johnny pushed Merilee until she almost slid off the orange plastic bench. "Your dad won't care. I'll practice double tomorrow."

Outside Theresa's Johnny started laughing and shaking his head. "Liar, liar, pants on fire."

LaDonna burst into laughter. "You noticed."

"How many basketball games have you ever attended with your dad, LaDonna? Huh? How many, huh?"

"Let's see." LaDonna pretended to count on her fingers. She laughed again. "I had to do something. I'd lost my appetite."

"There's always a hot dog at Mustard's Last Stand. I'm not going to let you get out of buying. It's not often you volunteer."

"That sounds like a perfectly healthy dinner, JB. Let's take them over into Central Park. We can look at the train and pretend we're going to Paris."

"Paris by train. Gotcha." Johnny grabbed her hand and they jogged together out to Broadway. Then they settled into a leisurely walk, neither saying anything until they reached the tiny diner at the bottom of the hill.

By the time they'd eaten and Johnny walked her home, her dad had gone someplace. LaDonna stared at the phone on the wall in the kitchen. Why not? She dug into her pocket for the phone number that Mrs. Coombs had written for her, smoothed the paper, dialed.

"Hello?" The voice was tentative, as if this girl was afraid to answer the phone.

"Minette Waterson?"

"Yes?"

"You don't know me. My name is La-Donna Martindale. I took the job at the art building that you tried to do. I—I just wondered why it was you quit so soon."

"Why do you want to know?" The girl's voice was somewhat defiant.

"Curiosity I guess. It doesn't matter if you'd rather not say." Now it did matter. LaDonna hoped Minette would keep talking.

"I—that basement is creepy. I felt scared down there alone. That's all. I didn't need the money *that* bad."

Silence. What Minette said gave La-Donna no further information.

"Don't tell me you like working there."

"It's okay." LaDonna laughed. "But that basement room is pretty scary."

"It's a creepy place and I never want to go down there again. Good luck."

"Thanks. Thanks for sharing your experience." LaDonna hung up and stared at the phone, not at all satisfied with the conversation.

"I guess, thanks," she said to the kitchen cabinets. She wanted to know why Minette felt scared, what she felt. She wished she had found the girl and talked to her in person. She opened the door to the refrigerator, stared inside at the cold white walls, the empty space. Her mind drifted. What was she doing? She wasn't hungry. But she grabbed a Coke.

The lid on the drink popped with a hiss. LaDonna walked slowly to her room and pulled out a sketch pad. From memory, she was able to reproduce, in an amateur-ish way, the painting he'd put on her wall. She studied it, tried to decide what it meant. Did it matter? She was successful in tapping into the emotional quality of the composition. Despite the overwhelming somber tones, there was an element of hope in the yellow light. She decided the robed figures were waiting for something or someone. Maybe that someone was coming from the storm, out of the storm, or despite the threatening fury of the sky.

It didn't matter what the painting said, but she enjoyed the exercise. For a few minutes she sketched her own emotions with a piece of charcoal, trying to be as free as possible—to free associate, letting her feelings come through her hand. Not thinking, just feeling what appeared on the page.

What she had when she finished was the best drawing she'd done in weeks. It wasn't great, but it was a start. Maybe— did she dare hope—she was moving past the block in her work.

The next day, she took her sketch pad to school. Spent all her free time doing the same free association doodling. By the time she got to sixth period she had six sketches, the last one somewhat finished.

Robby laid them out across a table and stared at them. He kept staring until La-Donna felt her stomach tighten, her underarms grow damp. She bit her bottom lip and looked at them with the teacher.

Eric Hunter stopped before Roddy said anything. He looked at all the sketches. "The work of a disturbed mind, I'd say." He laughed and winked at LaDonna. Never in her whole life had a boy winked at her. She didn't think she liked the gesture.

"Hunter, will you step into my office?"

Roddy said, his voice low and unemotional. "I'd like to talk to you for a few minutes."

"Sure, teach." Hunter gave LaDonna a parting grin.

"Sometimes they send me some real losers," Roddy mumbled, loud enough so that only LaDonna heard it. She felt it better not to comment.

"These are strong, emotional sketches, LaDonna. You may be onto something here. This may be your leap of faith. How about transferring this last, more finished one, to your canvas? Try painting it." Roddy shuffled the newsprint pages together with the picture he meant on top.

On canvas, the picture looked crude and stiff. Artificial. Even childlike. LaDonna stared at it, rolled her paint brush over and over from hand to hand. She couldn't bring herself to squeeze one dab of paint onto her palette.

Only once, during the hour, did she look at Johnny. She had walked to school early this morning, deliberately missing him. She felt a bit foolish about last night.

Her apprehension, however, paralleled an eagerness to get to the art building on campus, to the basement room. Would there be another painting? A note back from him, answering hers?

A good twenty minutes before the class was over, she packed up her fishing tackle box of paint tubes and brushes. Stuck the canvas board in her tote bag, along with her sketches. Turned, and without a word to anyone, left school through the back door.

If Roddy needed to tell her that her behavior was unacceptable, he could do so tomorrow. If Johnny thought she was being weird, she'd explain later.

She practically ran across the parking lot, over the bridge that spanned the creek behind the school, and up a short cut path to the college.

At the door to the art building, she paused. Took several deep breaths, her eyes closed, her mind blank.

Mrs. Coombs was on the phone and waved to her. LaDonna waved back, but she didn't stop to talk as she did occasionally. She needed to turn in her hours so she could get paid, but she'd do that later. All she really needed to do was slide a paper under the office door.

Closing the hall door behind her, she snapped on the stair light, thumped down, making plenty of noise. Did she have to warn him that she was coming? No, he'd know.

Deliberately, she dumped her stuff on the table, not looking at the walls. She steadied her shaking body, breathed in and out three more times, enjoying the musty smell of the room. And a faint hint of oil paint? Or was she imagining that?

Slowly she turned and stared at the

wall where the painting had appeared yesterday. It was still there. Another hung beside it. A note was slid into the corner of the frame of the first.

She grabbed it, clinching her fist around the paper until it crumbled and the cream-colored note floated gracefully to the floor. She snatched it up, held it more gingerly. The paper seemed really old, the ink watery and uneven.

How many works of art have you seen, LaDonna?

The connection took a few seconds. She had called his first painting a work of art.

She slapped open her notebook, tore out a sheet of tablet paper.

Some. Roddy took us to an exhibit at the Museum of Modern Art in New York. And I know what I like.

When she had scribbled that much, she stopped, sat on the hard, straight chair, and studied the second piece.

The style was similar. Those deep set eyes, lined with a thick, dark brown line. A child's face—a waif was a better word—certainly a child who was hungry, perhaps homeless, maybe without parents, a child stared at the horizon. There was the same stormy sky, the same empty horizon. But from the sky came a hint of light, celestial light?

Are you looking for something, too? Has anything ever appeared on the horizon for you?

"Very good," a low voice whispered from behind her.

She swung around. Then stood and backed up until her shoulders pressed against one wall of the warm room. "Who are you?" she asked in a soft voice. "Where are you?"

"Does it matter?" The voice seemed to be all around her. It bounced gently off the concrete walls, the plaster ceiling, the worn concrete floor.

"I—I guess not. I didn't imagine you, did I? You're the one who's been here all along."

"Do you think you're imagining me?"

"Stop answering my questions with another question." She felt some annoyance, some impatience with him, combined with a struggle of her lungs to suck in enough air, which suggested she was also afraid.

She didn't want to be afraid. "Should I be afraid of you?"

"What do you think? Have you been afraid until now? For three weeks? Are you afraid now?"

"Some." She licked her lips. Her mouth felt cottony. She sucked her cheeks to find enough saliva to swallow. Then she caught one cheek in her teeth and bit down just enough to be sure she was awake. Of course she was awake.

"I'm glad you came," he said. "I was lonely."

"What do you want?"

"Your company. What do you want?"

He did it again. Asked another question in response to hers. She forced herself to relax. He was the same person. The only thing that had changed was his speaking to her. Why should she be afraid now? "I want to paint again. I've been blocked. Do you ever get blocked?" She'd talk to him as she would any artist. As she would Roddy.

"Of course. All artists get blocked. So do writers. It's part of the business."

"How about pianists?" she asked just for fun.

"They get strung out, nervous, hard to live with. Everything they play sounds off key."

"How do you know this?"

"I watch people. I know what they're feeling."

"You've been watching me for three weeks." She looked in every corner of the room. There wasn't any place to hide. She didn't have the nerve to open either door to or from the room. "What am I feeling?"

"Frustration. Maybe you could paint here. I might be able to help you. It's worth a try."

"That wouldn't be fair. I'm supposed to be working for Glen Walker. For the gallery."

"No one is monitoring you. Don't turn in the hours when you're painting. This work you're doing here is not very valuable anyway. You're the only one in this room with any talent."

"Besides you." She felt comfortable enough to tease.

"I guess I was talented."

"Was?"

"Am."

LaDonna needed no more encouragement. She set out her canvas board, wishing she had her easel, but she could paint without it. She clicked open the dark green fishing tackle box with its small compartments, each filled with tubes of paint of varying sizes.

With no more thinking, she set to work.

She had no idea how much time had passed until she looked at her watch. It was midnight. But a painting was finished.

She realized now that she had never questioned what colors to use, what brush strokes or brush size, how much paint to apply. She seemed to know.

She was pleased with the picture except for one thing. "It looks like something you painted."

She spoke to him again without stopping to feel if he was there. She got no answer. And she was incredibly tired.

She'd leave the picture on the table to dry, and for him to look at. Maybe he'd leave her a note about how to improve it. Maybe he'd say what he thought of it.

Please tell me what you think.

She left him a note.

From the middle of the room, she pulled off the light, stood for a minute in the darkness. It was velvety. She took it in, surrounded by a feeling of well being. He really wasn't there, but it was all right. This was her place, too. A place she could hide, she realized. A place where she could shut out the world, feel safe, feel totally accepted.

"Goodbye," she whispered, as much to the room as to him.

At the top of the stairs, she looked back into the pit of darkness. The black hole invited her back. She smiled. "Later."

The upstairs hall was another matter. The building was empty she knew. Her footsteps echoed behind her. And she realized she was going to have to cross the campus and get home at a very late hour. Her trip to Old Main last night to find Johnny flashed into her mind. The idea that someone had followed her.

For the first time ever, she was afraid of the darkness.

57

six

LaDonna PAUSED AT the front door of the art building, then tried to push it open. It seemed extra heavy but it wasn't locked from the inside. She leaned into it, barely forcing it wide enough to slide out.

While she was painting in the basement the weather had changed. A wild, twisting wind storm roared across the campus in full force.

Trees bent their full-leafed limbs in protest. Savage gusts rustled the young leaves, tore them from their stems, tossed them through the air. The storm sent small limbs sailing, swept dirt and trash through the turbulent air.

Grit filled her eyes the minute she faced east. Tears blurred her vision as she blinked and blinked. Her thin jacket slapped and billowed, the wind threatening to rip it off and send it westward. Gathering the bottom in both hands, she managed to zip it closed. Now it was plastered to her body, offering no warmth. An icy edge to the wind knifed through her body, twisted and loosened her braid, sweeping curls away from her face. Then her hair whipped back, stinging her face.

Instead of walking toward Broadway, she cut north, even though that path took her through the trees. She didn't feel very safe walking under them, but the route was shorter. Sometimes these storms uprooted whole trunks that had stood for years. Huge limbs cracked and snapped like twigs.

Inclement weather lured LaDonna outside to take long walks. Rain, snow gently falling, provided a solitude she loved, and she sometimes roamed for miles, returning to the house soaked and satisfied. This wind was not friendly, or inviting.

She had forgotten to be afraid until she heard the thudding footfalls behind her, coming fast. She turned and just had time to throw out both arms to catch the body hurling towards her.

"Oh! Let go! Leave me alone!" The woman started to beat LaDonna with her fists, to struggle and thrash about wildly.

"Hey, hey, hey, stop that. You're all right. I'm not going to hurt you. What's

59

wrong?" LaDonna clasped her in a bear hug to stop her hysterics.

The young woman, tall and thin, but strong, sagged against LaDonna. Her weight was too much and LaDonna let her sink to the sidewalk. She crouched beside the girl, cradling her until she calmed enough to speak.

Instead of talking, the girl began to cry. LaDonna sat down and waited. No way could she leave the woman alone until she found out why she was so distraught.

As the two huddled, the wind swept around them, but it was less violent under the pines. The moaning and whistling distanced itself, leaving them in a small pocket of quiet.

Finally her sobbing and puppy whimpers ceased and the woman bent double. She slid her knees up, circled them with both arms, buried her face, gasped, coughed, and sucked in air. LaDonna waited, patting the woman's shoulder to reassure her that she was okay. That she was with a friend.

"Better?" LaDonna finally said.

"I'm okay now. Thanks." The woman raised her head, wiped her eyes with the sleeve of her warm-up suit.

"I'll never, never run across the campus at night again."

"You were out running in this storm?" LaDonna knew Bellponte was full of fanatics who ran in snow, rain, freezing cold.

"The wind wasn't blowing when I left home. I ran to the campus. Planned to get a book at the library and run back home."

"And what happened? What frightened you?"

"Someone was following me."

"Are you sure?" LaDonna looked around, but they were alone.

"He grabbed me when I came out of the library and headed toward Old Main. I hadn't started running yet. I was zipping the book into my jacket."

"I thought you were awfully flat-chested." Maybe teasing her would help her relax.

She did laugh a little. "Yeah, but if I'd have kept the book in my hand, I could have hit him with it."

"But you got away?" LaDonna wanted the rest of the story. The woman's experience made her realize that maybe she hadn't been spooked for nothing the other night.

"I twisted out of his hold. Kicked him in the stomach. Maybe he hadn't expected me to be so strong. Hey, thanks." She got to her feet. "I hope I didn't scare you too bad."

"I was a bit startled when I turned around and saw you hurling towards me. I think someone was following me up here the other night. This makes me angry. I've never been afraid before. But then I've never wandered around the campus at night before. I just got a job up here." LaDonna rattled on, suddenly needing to talk.

"Listen, which way were you headed? Could I walk with you? I doubt if he followed me far. I can outrun almost anyone. I'm on the track and field team."

"Maybe I should think again about the benefits of pounding the pavement every day." All LaDonna would do was think about running. She wasn't the least bit athletic. "I'm going towards College Avenue, but I'll go whichever way you need to go until we get to busier streets."

"That's perfect. I live down off of Twentieth. I had planned to run down Seventeenth, but when I took off, I had no sense of which way I was headed. I never walk by this pond."

They skirted the edge of the Varsity Pond, and the woman looked back several times. When they reached College, the wind roared again, pushing them along.

"My name's Mary Lou Shoemaker. You a freshman?" Mary Lou felt recovered enough for small talk.

"Actually I'm a high school senior. I got a job on the campus, and hope it will continue next year when I do go to the college. I'm an artist." It was the first time

LaDonna had said that in a long time—well, she used to say, I'm going to be an artist. She realized the difference.

"I'm impressed. I don't have any talents."

"Except running." LaDonna joked again.

Mary Lou was able to laugh. "Yeah, you're right. I guess that is a talent. I may even think about the Olympics. The competition is incredibly hard work, but once you win one of those medals, no one can ever take that away from you. You're in the books forever."

"I guess so. I've never thought about winning anything."

"You any good? As an artist, I mean?"

"I—I think I am. It takes a lot of self-confidence."

"Don't let anyone stop you, girl. If that's what you want. Don't let anyone say you can't."

"Someone tonight said I could." LaDonna just remembered what he'd said. "He said I had a lot of talent."

"Then believe him. You're lucky if even one person believes in you. But believe in yourself. No one else will very often. To tell the truth, no one else will care very much. I'm the only one who thinks I should try for the Olympics. 'That's hard work, girl. And losing will break your heart. Don't even try.' That's what *my* friends say. They know they wouldn't do it."

Mary Lou stopped in front of a huge old house, probably divided into several apartments. "I live here. Thanks."

"Nice running into you." LaDonna shook Mary Lou's hand. "I can say, I know her, when your picture is in the paper or you're on TV accepting that medal."

"And I'll get so many jobs advertising shoes and running clothes I'll be able to afford one of your paintings. It's a deal, okay?" Mary Lou grinned.

"Okay."

"You afraid to go the rest of the way to your place?"

"Not now."

"Then take care."

A bond had formed between the two women. They might never meet again, but LaDonna felt close to Mary Lou Shoemaker. They shared something in common. A yearning. A dream of being more than most people dared go for.

As she stepped onto the porch of her own house, LaDonna recognized a sense of excitement she hadn't had in a long time. She thought of the painting she'd left in the basement room. *Please, please let it be as good as I think it is. Please, please let the block be gone. I need to believe in myself again.*

Mary Lou was right. It didn't matter how many people did or didn't believe in you. You had to believe in yourself.

She could hardly wait until tomorrow. She'd go up to the campus on her noon hour—cut a class if she needed to—and get her picture. If it wasn't good, she'd do another. And another.

Maybe the wind had done her a favor. It had blown away the little dark cloud she'd let stop over her head.

Roddy would be glad to see her recover her confidence, return to her old self.

Johnny would celebrate with her. She'd helped him live through some of his gloomy gray clouds.

And *he*—he would be glad, she thought. He'd be especially glad.

seven

THE NEXT MORNING LaDonna lay in bed for a few minutes, remembering. What she really wanted to do was to jump up, dress, and run to the art building. See if she really did paint something new. See if she still liked it. There wasn't time now. She'd make herself wait until noon.

She stretched, crawled out of bed, and, wrapped in a towel, headed for the hall bathroom. She wished she had her own bath, but the small house only had one bathroom and shower.

Dressing was easy. She had a sort of uniform she wore every day. Clothes weren't important to her, plus she had little money to spend on extras. Buying paint really did take all she could scrape together. Jeans, tee-shirt or sweatshirt, depending on the season, sometimes an old shirt over the tee. The old shirt was usually paint-spotted. So were the jeans.

When she became a famous artist, would she dress differently? She daydreamed while she made her bed and gathered her books and notebooks. She might wear exotic gowns, or flowing wide pants of silk. She might design her own clothes and have someone sew them for her. But just for openings and parties. In her studio she'd look just like she did now. She'd continue to braid her hair in one braid, since it curled on its own and was out of control if she didn't do something. It escaped all around her face in clean blond wisps. She hated dirty hair and always kept hers sparkling. She hoped that balanced out her limited wardrobe.

In the kitchen, her father sprawled at the table, a cup of coffee in one hand, the newspaper spread before him. He looked as if he'd just come from work.

"You on the night shift now, Daddy?" she asked, just to be polite.

"Yes." He sipped the coffee. "It's just awful."

"I thought you liked working at night so you could go to the day games." Her father's voice sounded awful. Its tone made LaDonna have a little empathy for him.

"No, this." He pushed the *Bellponte Daily* towards her.

She wished she'd never have looked. But who could avoid the huge picture and the screaming headlines.

CAMPUS COED BRUTALLY MURDERED

And the smaller type underneath.

Body Found In Practice Room

The photo was of one of the practice rooms at Old Main. It was horribly blood-splattered, and the sight sent shivers over LaDonna. Her stomach turned over and threatened to spill out the few sips of coffee she'd taken, the half bagel.

She didn't want to read on, but she did.

When young, promising pianist, John Blair, went to find Katherine Taylor, planning to walk her to her campus room, he found instead her body and grisly evidence of foul play.

After lengthy questioning, Blair stayed with his story. It seems Katherine had interrupted him some two hours earlier saying she thought she had been followed across campus. She was nervous about walking home alone, so Blair volunteered his company when she was ready to leave.

Blair, a high school senior, studies piano at the college, and so uses the practice room on a regular basis as did Taylor, a junior music major at Bellponte.

An all-night search by the police found no other evidence. Bellponte coroner placed the time of death as soon after Taylor had talked to Blair. Blair is not being held at this time, and police have no suspects.

"Well, I hope not." LaDonna bit her lip and blinked back tears. "They can't think Johnny killed her, can they, Dad?"

"They can think anything they please." Her father cupped both hands around his coffee mug and stared into the creamy liquid. "They can think I did it."

"Were you there? Is that your building?" LaDonna hadn't even considered that her father was a suspect, too. She didn't much like him, or invite his company, but he wasn't a murderer. Was he? The most curious sense of not knowing her father at all took hold of her.

Without meaning to, wanting to, she drew back into herself. Stared at her father with new eyes. He was rumpled, bleary eyed, needed a shave. He was also overweight. She certainly couldn't imagine him running after someone on campus, or even hurrying after them. He moved at a turtle's pace in everything he did.

"Did they question you? Did you see anything?" LaDonna just kept tossing out her own questions.

"The story is all in there." Her father pushed the newspaper towards LaDonna. She read on to find her father's name.

Janitor Sam Martindale was also questioned. According to his story, he arrived at Old Main after the time of Taylor's death, but cleaned only the main floor. He saw nothing, heard nothing. Since the practice rooms are sound proof, the possibility of anyone hearing Taylor's screams for help is slim.

LaDonna's mind flew to Mary Lou Shoemaker running across the campus. Had Mary Lou gotten up to see this headline? Realized this murderer may have been the same person who followed her? She should call the police. Maybe LaDonna should call them, too.

She'd wait. She jumped up. "I'm going to school, Dad. See you later."

Where she was going was to Johnny's house. She flew out the door to find it raining. Stepping back inside, she grabbed a hooded jacket, slipped it on, then half walked, half ran to the Blairs' house, only a block from hers.

"Is Johnny here?" she asked the sleepy woman who opened the door.

"Hi, LaDonna. He's still at breakfast. Aren't you early?"

"Yes. But I was worried about him."

LaDonna brushed past Mrs. Blair and ran to the kitchen.

Johnny was slumped over the newspaper. He glanced up at LaDonna, but said nothing. His hair stuck up all whichaway. His eyes were red. A stubble of golden fuzz fringed his chin. LaDonna was sure he hadn't slept.

"Johnny, I'm so sorry." She was sorry she'd felt the least bit jealous of Katherine and Johnny. She knew it was silly, but now it seemed even worse. "You've been up all night, haven't you?" She stood beside him, touched his shoulder.

He nodded. "They made me tell my story over and over. Like I was a suspect. Like I could kill—kill—her." Johnny acted as if he couldn't call Katherine's name. Like if he didn't, this wouldn't be her, dead.

"I know, Johnny, I know. They questioned my father, too. They're desperate to find the killer. They don't really believe you killed her. They couldn't."

"I think they could." Johnny's clothes were all wrinkled as if he'd slept in them. Had he even gone to bed?

"Don't go to school, Johnny. You need some sleep. I'll stop at the office and tell them."

"Think you'll have to?" Now Johnny's voice sounded bitter. "Why did they have to print this photo? It was awful, La-

Donna, just awful. I went there, expecting—expecting to—"

"I know, Johnny, I know. You don't have to explain it to me. It's a terrible thing to have to see." She hugged him, cradling his head against her waist, feeling his crisp curly hair, the stubble of beard across his face.

"You want some company? I could cut classes, too." She moved away from him, sat in one of the hard kitchen chairs.

Taking both of his hands in hers, she squeezed the long, strong fingers, staring at the close-cut nails, kept short for the piano. The tip of each finger was slightly calloused from seeking out the keys, from playing his music over and over until it was perfect. She had watched him play. He retreated into himself, caressed the piano, coaxing the melody from a black and white keyboard. If Johnny Blair even had a wife, she would come second to his music. His love affair would always be with his own compositions and composers long dead.

Johnny shook his head. "No. Thanks, though, LaDonna."

She sat there a few minutes more. Shook her head no when Mrs. Blair offered her coffee.

Reluctantly she left. She walked slowly to Bellponte High, detouring around twisted limbs on the sidewalk. Drifts of leaves, branches, the aftermath of the night's wind storm.

She found herself a celebrity because Johnny wasn't there. Everyone knew they were friends. Everyone asked her about Johnny. She didn't bother to answer, just whirled and walked away. Inside her chest, a wild storm of her own built. People never spoke to her. Now they wanted gossip.

By ten o'clock, she'd had enough. Slamming her books into her locker, she marched out of the building. Let a teacher stop her. Let someone ask where she was going. She was eager to unleash her anger on whoever dared.

She reached the art building with no interference. Did she expect the campus to be swarming with uniformed searchers? What would they be looking for? They'd found her body. Any other evidence would have blown all the way to Canada last night.

There was no one in the art office to stop her. She hurried to the basement door, paused before it. Did she really want to hide out here? She didn't know where else to go. She certainly wasn't going home.

Stepping slowly onto each step, she listened to the groans and creaks, heard the old building whispering a welcome.

The gallery, as she had started calling

it once she'd hung paintings, held a dim, smoky light at mid-morning. The smell of oil paint greeted her nostrils. She inhaled it gratefully. It was like a drug, one that calmed. Like Johnny's music, her art was a place to retreat, to hide if you wanted to say that, to forget that a world where people could kill another human being existed.

She sat. Stared at the painting she had finished last night. The composition, the work was far superior to anything she had ever painted before. Had she really painted it herself? Maybe he had painted it. The style imitated his. She saw that at once. The eyes were dark as if smudged in with a thumbprint of kohl. The long, strong fingers of the child stretched, exaggerated because he was reaching. Reaching for what? The empty sky? The bare, lonely horizon? One had to imagine what he yearned for, but the yearning was on his face. Tears came into her eyes looking at the child. This was the first time she had captured such emotion in a painting. That made her question even more whether or not she'd achieved this level of work.

"It's good, isn't it?" The voice was low, silken, and it held a note of admiration.

"You painted it, didn't you? The style is like yours."

He laughed. "You think I painted that?

I watched you paint it. Maybe I leaned over your shoulder, but you held the brush."

Inadvertently, she glanced behind her. "Who are you? Where are you? Why can't I see you?"

"Angry are we? Why are you angry, La-Donna Martindale?"

She rubbed the frown line between her eyebrows. Bit her lip. "I—I'm not mad at you."

"I know that. I know everything."

"You know who killed her?"

"Let that go, LaDonna. It doesn't concern you."

"It does, too. They think Johnny did it."

"What do you think?"

"Johnny couldn't do such a thing."

"Go with your heart, your passion." He was silent for a few moments while La-Donna studied her painting. "Your passion went into this painting. You see that, don't you?"

"Yes. But I've imitated your style. You see that, don't you?" She still felt a grain of anger rubbing her, irritating her emotions into a bitter pearl of gray ice.

"There's nothing wrong with that. A student often imitates her teacher. Look at all the old masters. Their students imitated them. That's why there were schools of painting. All the Impressionists have similarities. Look at what followed Picasso's lead."

"Are you my teacher now?" She smiled, rather liking the idea.

"Would that please you?"

"I—I guess so. Who are you?"

"The night. You like the night.

> *'Night, sable goddess from her ebony throne*
> *In rayless majesty, now stretches forth*
> *Her leaden septre o'er a slum'ring world.'* "

"You're a poet, too?" She smiled, running her fingers across the rough-textured painting. She'd used a palette knife for some parts, piling on paint for depth.

"Edward Young. One of my favorite poets. I only paint."

"If you won't tell me your name, I'm going to call you Mr. Sable. Night artist in this dark gallery."

"Now *you're* waxing poetic. And you're in pain. Paint from that pain."

"Right now?"

"Do you want to return to school?"

"No. I can't."

She slid another canvas board from her bag, prepared earlier with a wash of white gesso. She stared at the whiteness, the absence of color, emotion, passion. She let it hypnotize her until she reached deep inside herself. Without thought she dipped her brush into the black paint.

When she came out of her deep trance, that intense concentration she'd found the night before, she stared at the painting. A body slumped on a street curb just off center, curled into itself, blond head tucked into knees, arms circling legs, as if holding the body together. She imagined the body flying off in all directions, broken pieces strewing the street if it weren't wrapped tightly. Long fingers bit into the leg flesh, holding tightly like the straps on a trunk, long sealed up, hiding a secret. The sky was leaden, threatening, as if it could easily swallow up the figure.

She'd alternated color on a corner of the brick building so that it imitated piano keys. But probably she was the only one who would see that in the painting.

"That's your friend, isn't it?" The low voice spoke for the first time. There had been no verbal communication while she painted, but now that she was aware, she thought she had probably felt his presence while she worked.

"He's in pain."

"You've captured it well."

"Did—did you help me?"

"Do you think I did?"

"I don't know."

Had he guided her hand? Was this his work or hers? Did it matter? A sudden fit of laughter bubbled up.

"What am I going to tell Roddy, Mr.

Sable? That a ghost helped me paint these new pictures. That I was heavily influenced by two paintings that have appeared on the wall in my dark gallery?" She laughed out loud.

"Tell him they came from inside you. That side that is sensitive to others. You can't escape the world around you."

"How do you know?"

"I tried."

"Tell me about it." She cleaned her brushes, easing the creamy acrylic paint from the soft bristles.

"It doesn't matter now."

"What if it matters to me?"

"Then you'll know sometime." He left. She felt him go.

"Mr. Sable!" She stood and whirled around. "Why did you leave? I'm sorry I pried. I won't ask questions. I don't really care who are you. I don't care about anything but your art. My painting." She stared into the dim corners. Even walked over and opened the other door. It was the first time she'd opened that door. Something had kept her from doing so.

A dark musty smell floated over her, around her. Cold, dry darkness, empty. Goose bumps raised on her arms. Icy air stabbed her stomach. Pain—his pain. Loneliness—his loneliness.

She slammed the door, wanted to lock

it, but there was no key in the small narrow slot under the cold brass knob.

Please don't be really gone, she thought. Promise me you'll be back.

She got no answer. She gathered her paints and last night's painting. She left a final thought message. *I'll be back tonight. Please be here.*

She couldn't imagine losing him.

eight

LaDONNA DASHED DOWN the hill, took the short cut to the high school, and was able to get back to school in time for art class. She took last night's painting—had she only finished this last night? So much had happened it seemed weeks ago. She took the canvas board and placed it on her easel while people wandered into class and got settled. She stared at it, making sure she wanted Roddy to see it.

Yes, she was still pleased. In this light, the lack of color was even more effective. Dark stood out from light in a perfect balance.

She felt Roddy standing behind her before he spoke. "Did you paint this, La-Donna?" Roddy didn't believe the painting was hers either. What should she tell him?

"I—I—yes, late last night." She had placed the paint on the canvas. Where the inspiration came from was still an unknown, and there was no way she could explain it to Mr. Rodriguez.

"It's—it's wonderful. It has such emotion, something your paintings have lacked. What inspired you?" Roddy reached out carefully and touched some of the lines, ran his finger across the horizon.

"I've been looking at a lot of art work. I found a couple of paintings that I really liked, that touched me. I—I—imitated their style a little. Do you think that's all right? To imitate someone's style that you admire?"

"Of course, LaDonna. Sometimes we call that echoing. Music composers do it all the time, echo a phrase from an early symphony or concerto. Painters have been doing the same thing for all of time. Experts have looked at paintings and wondered if an old master painted it— Rembrandt for instance, but they suspect it was the work of one of his students. Whose paintings were you studying?"

"I'd rather not say."

Roddy didn't press her. "Well, whoever it was, it was a fortunate happening. Something in his work touched you, enabled you to take that leap of painting with emotion yourself. Emotion was really what was lacking in your work, LaDonna. I've just now realized it. I think you've taught me something. I tell students to paint from their hearts, but I can't show them how to do that."

"I have a confession to make, Roddy."

"I'll never tell." He turned and smiled at her and there was pride in that smile. LaDonna took it in. She realized she badly needed Roddy's praise.

"I cut classes this morning. People were pestering me about Johnny. Asking me questions since he wasn't here to talk for himself. I couldn't take it. I went—I went home and painted another picture. I'll bring it in tomorrow."

"Did you paint it with the anger that made you leave school?" He guessed her emotion.

"No, I painted from Johnny's pain. I talked to him this morning. Then I put myself inside of him when I worked."

"You've made that leap, LaDonna. I think you've found that magic place, deep inside yourself. That place where art comes from. Wadsworth calls it 'the inner vision.' That place where all your senses are involved."

All LaDonna's senses and emotions had been so involved this morning that she couldn't take it, she realized. That was why she had left school. The murder of Katherine Taylor sickened her. Johnny's pain was her pain. Mary Lou's fear had echoed her fear of the night before.

"I wish I could have discovered that place without Katherine being murdered," LaDonna said in a low voice. She didn't want any of the class to hear her, to join in this conversation.

"You knew her?"

"Not really. But I had met her. That room was near where Johnny practices. He introduced me to her."

"I understand your feelings, LaDonna." Roddy touched her shoulder, something he'd rarely done before, observing the unwritten rule of teachers not touching students, even those who so badly needed the touch of a friendly hand. "I could be called a Pollyanna, but I like to think life has balance. That good can come from evil. If your finding that inner eye within yourself from which you can create paintings like this came from Katherine's death, that can be some comfort to you."

"I would never have thought of that, Roddy. I'd like to feel that way. Thanks for sharing your feelings, your thoughts about this."

"That's what teachers are for." He changed his tone of voice to teasing. She had seldom heard him serious for long.

"Roddy." She could tease, too. "You said something in *his* work touched me.

My other teacher. How do you know it was a he?"

"My sincere apology, LaDonna. I try to be politically correct. Something in *his or her* work touched you. Was the artist you have taken as mentor female?"

She grinned. "No, but I just wanted you to admit it could have been."

"Done. When will you bring your second work in?"

"Tomorrow. It was still wet."

"I'll look forward to seeing it. Now get started on another right now." Roddy moved to stand behind Merilee Morris, who was staring at them, her eyes red, as if she had been crying. LaDonna wondered if Merilee had bought into Eric Hunter's flirting ways only to get hurt when she realized he came on to all women that way.

Not my problem, she thought. She set the painting of the yearning child on the floor in front of her easel. She prepared another canvas board, a bigger one this time. Then she stood and stared at it. The blank canvas stared back. She had read about writers facing a white page every morning, or maybe now a blank computer screen. This must be the same feeling.

She had no feeling left, she realized. She had completely emptied her emotions into the picture she'd painted in the basement room. Or—or—she didn't want to complete her thought.

Eric Hunter kept her from having to, and at the same time restored her strong feelings. He stood staring at the picture on the floor. Then he leaned over and picked it up. She didn't want him to touch it, but it was too late.

He leaned it on her easel, ignoring the wet white gesso. Stepping back, he caught his chin between his thumb and first finger. She held her breath, not meaning to, not wanting to care what he thought of her work.

"*You* painted this?"

His tone of voice said she didn't. Said he didn't believe that she had. The statement restored her own doubts, but she would never admit them to Eric.

"Are you saying I didn't?" Her voice was sharp, but controlled. She *didn't* care what he thought.

"The style looks really familiar. I've seen pictures a lot like it before."

"The Mexican painter Orozco painted in a similar style. Maybe that's what you're seeing."

"I don't know his work," Eric admitted.

"In order to paint or teach you should have a wide knowledge of other painters." Slam dunk. She loved criticizing him.

He never even noticed the sharp twist

of her knife. Some really sensitive guy we have here, wanting to paint and teach art, she thought.

"Who did you copy?" He swung around and stared at her. "Where did you find a picture like this?" His eyes were steel gray daggers, nailing her to the table behind her. She was surprised at the emotion in his voice.

"I resent what you're saying, Mr.—" She caught herself. They had given him so many nicknames behind his back, she nearly called him another name without meaning to. "Mr. Hunter. I painted this picture. And tomorrow I'll have another. You're out of line."

She took the picture and, wrapping it in a soft dry paint rag, placed it in her tote bag.

"I hope you didn't learn your teaching skills, your method of criticizing a student's work at Bellponte College. I plan to study there next year, and I'd hate to think the teachers are anything like you." She minced no words in cutting him down. She had a great deal of respect for Mr. Rodriguez. She had none, she owed none, to Eric Hunter.

For the second time that day, she left school. Only a few minutes before the class was over, but she realized she couldn't paint any more today anyway, especially in the art room. With Eric

Hunter looking over her shoulder. Doubting. That would be the way to shut up his accusations. To let her watch her compose a similar picture. But it was useless.

She was going to Johnny's house. She was suddenly worried about Johnny Blair. A strong, deep concern sent her towards his house, almost at a run.

nine

HER INSTINCTS WERE right. Johnny was upset. His mother was glad to let LaDonna in. "I hope you can talk him into practicing. He's not very good company right now." Mrs. Blair smiled and pointed towards the next room. LaDonna thought she was probably used to Johnny's moods, but she seemed concerned about him as well.

Johnny spoke as soon as he saw La-Donna, as if he was really saying, go away, don't bug me about this. "I can't go back up there, LaDonna. I keep thinking about that room, about Katherine." Johnny sat staring out the family room picture window at the rain that had started gently falling, the rain that was predicted to turn to snow by night. A

flock of small birds, knowing the weather was changing, fed frantically at the bird feeder. Flames danced as fire crackled in the fireplace.

"You have to, Johnny. You need that piano. This one just isn't the same." La-Donna indicated the old-fashioned upright that Johnny had started playing on when he was five. She fingered a few keys. The instrument had a lovely tone, but nothing like the baby grand in the practice room.

She sat on the bench for a few minutes, keeping Johnny company in his misery. Maybe she had the solution.

"I'll go with you. I'll stay in the room and listen to you practice."

"You don't want to do that. You'll get bored. I'd worry about you being there, getting bored." Johnny splayed the fingers of both hands, long slender fingers, and looked at them as if they held the answer to his dilemma.

LaDonna knew that after about five minutes Johnny wouldn't worry about her. He wouldn't know she was there. "I never get bored with your music, Johnny. But if I do, I'll tell you. We can go get that pizza I promised."

Johnny thought about that for a time. Finally he stood up. "Okay. I'm going nuts sitting around here."

Now Mrs. Blair worried about them getting wet. She insisted they take two umbrellas and that LaDonna borrow her raincoat.

Outside, lowering her umbrella and sharing Johnny's, LaDonna laughed. "I don't know if I could take that much mothering. I'm so used to being independent."

"She means well." Johnny put his arm around LaDonna's waist to keep them together under the ribbed taffeta. LaDonna felt warm inside and out and as cozy as she had in the family room.

"She wants her baby to stay well for his recitals," she teased. "Are you playing in May?" Her plan was to distract him from everything except his music.

"Yes, and I'm nowhere near ready."

"You will be. You always are." They splashed in puddles until they climbed Seventeenth Street hill where water ran towards them in small rivers. "I'm painting again, Johnny. Good stuff. But Eric Hunter thinks it's not my work."

"That phony. He's probably envious. You realize we haven't seen any of his paintings. Or one sculpture. Whatever he does. You know how you feel about what you're doing. Ignore anything he says."

"I will. But I didn't like his saying this isn't my work or that I've copied something." LaDonna knew that one reason she hated what Eric said so much was that

she had her own doubts. She just couldn't shake them, believe entirely in herself.

Their silence as she and Johnny walked was comfortable. But when they reached Old Main, LaDonna felt Johnny tense. He lowered the umbrella and stepped away from her, entering the building. He stared at the staircase as if reluctant to start climbing.

"Race you." LaDonna leaped up the first steps, pounding ahead of Johnny. She heard him behind her. She kept running as far as she could. Then she gasped and slowed to a walk. "I never claimed to be athletic. You can win."

Johnny was panting, too. "You already beat me. I usually take the elevator."

"You don't!" LaDonna laughed, or tried to. Laughter seemed wrong up here.

On the third floor, Johnny hurried to his room, unlocked the door, and slid in, as if once inside he'd be safe from his awful memories. LaDonna knew he'd never be free of them, but she stayed right beside him and kept him talking.

"I'm not going to sit beside you. I'd be in the way. I'll just sit right here on the floor in the corner, Johnny, behind you. Is that okay? What are you working on?"

Johnny opened the bench. "Rachmaninoff. His Concerto in F Sharp Minor, Opus One. Everyone plays his second. He wrote this when he was about seventeen. I'm way behind." He set his music on the piano, plopped down on the bench, adjusted the bench, adjusted his shirt sleeves, wiggled to get comfortable. LaDonna figured his motions were ritual. He did this every time he sat down in order to get his mind and body ready.

She leaned against the corner wall, slid until she was on the wood floor. Stretching her legs in front of her, she wriggled until she was comfortable. Then she waited.

Johnny limbered his fingers with some scales and bits and pieces of runs and trills up and down the keyboard. Suddenly, his hands both came down hard, making her jump, then his fingers cascaded across chord after chord. Once he started to play the concerto, she was surrounded and caught up in the melody. He didn't need the music. He had the piece memorized. And in no time she knew he was unaware of her presence.

She was not unaware of Johnny Blair, however. He expressed the music with his whole body, leaning forward, straightening, leaning back, his face tilting up as if, like fine wine, he was savoring the notes he struck.

When the melody softened with a hint of nostalgia, Johnny's fingers caressed the keys. His hands arched, he raised them on and off the ivory with such grace, like gentle ocean waves slipping in and out on a quiet beach. Without meaning to, she imagined those same fingers caressing her face, her body. She shuddered with emotion.

Now with crashing waves, Johnny poured his heart into the piece. The music intensified as did her emotion. The low notes stirred her deep inside, pounding, churning, sending her into passion she had never even imagined.

A sudden realization flooded her. She was in love with Johnny Blair. She had been in love with him for all of time, their time, as short as it was, as few years as they had lived. She wanted to love him forever.

Pulling her legs up, she wrapped her arms around her knees, hugged herself into a small ball to contain her feelings. She realized she was imitating Johnny's position in her painting of him, but where in the picture Johnny was filled with pain, she was filled with love, with passion, with such a deep emotion that it both thrilled and frightened her.

She had to leave. Johnny couldn't know this—how she was feeling about him. She had no idea if he would return the emotion. She had no idea how he felt about her. They were friends, buddies. They had been friends forever, bonding together in mutual misery, driven by art and music, the need to express themselves with paint and melodies, and in no other way.

Crawling quietly, she moved toward the doorway. Could she leave without Johnny knowing? She didn't want him to stop playing. She didn't want to interrupt, intrude on this space he had entered. She had shared it. That was enough. And he had forgotten—for a short time. He was free of fear, of memory. He lived for this moment, and this moment only.

Placing her hand on the doorknob, she twisted it slowly, pulled, stepped into the hall, pulled it closed behind her. Then for a few seconds she leaned against the wall, breathing deeply.

Paint with your passion, your emotion. She heard Mr. Sable speak to her. Yes, she must go immediately to the basement art room. She must capture this emotion that filled her, threatened to spill over, to melt her whole body like candle wax. She must paint.

She turned and fled down the hall to the stairs. Halfway there she froze, staring, at seeing a familiar figure.

Her father leaned forward, his head pressing on the wall. He was crying.

ten

"DAD, IS THAT you?" She knew it was. She just didn't know what to say to him.

Her dad looked at her through teary eyes. "Donnie?"

He hadn't called her that since she was little—four or five. It touched her deeply, mixing with the well of emotion already filling her from Johnny's music, filling her, spilling out. She felt her own eyes water. She blinked to clear them.

"Dad, what's wrong?" She touched his shoulder. She couldn't remember the last time she had touched him.

"She was so beautiful—so beautiful. I was standing here remembering. She always spoke to me."

LaDonna stepped back. "Katherine?" For some reason, finding her father in the hall, this near the practice room where Katherine Taylor was murdered, didn't feel good to her once he had spoken her name.

"Yes, she was so beautiful."

A ring of keys hung at her father's belt. He would have access to any room in this building. Even a practice room that was locked. Locked without anyone in it. Locked from the inside by a student who was practicing. A student who didn't feel secure up here alone at night in an unlocked room.

"I was up here with Johnny." LaDonna felt compelled to tell her father what she was doing in The Tower, but not to stay here talking to him for long. "He's practicing the piano. And I'm going over to where I'm working to paint."

"Where is that?"

Had he forgotten? For some reason, LaDonna didn't want her father to know exactly where she was. "In the art building."

For some reason? She knew why. Her father was scaring her. The suspicion that had flitted through her mind, unbidden, was there now. She felt guilty about it, but it had surfaced, mainly because she realized she didn't know him really well. The idea of her father killing someone was absurd, but the idea had come to her. It would take some work on her part to make it go away.

"I'll see you later, unless you think you need to go home. Want me to drive you home, Dad?"

"Oh, no. I'll be all right in a minute." He dug in his pocket for a handkerchief. "I—I just thought of her again."

LaDonna was glad to leave, to escape. She pounded down the stairwell and out the front door of Old Main. Then she closed her eyes and took deep damp breaths of the rain-soaked air. She still had Mrs. Blair's cheery red umbrella. She raised it and walked quickly towards her basement room.

He was there. A new painting hung on the wall. This one was more cheerful. Red was the dominant color. A road disappeared on the horizon, a road bordered by fields of red flowers—poppies? But was it cheerful after all? The sky reflected the red flowers as it would an inferno, as if the fields blossomed with flames instead of flowers.

"At first I thought it was cheerful, but I changed my mind," LaDonna said out loud. "Is it anger or frustration?"

He laughed. "You're getting the idea. Each painting carries an emotion, touches an emotional chord in the viewer. You're ready to paint, aren't you?"

The emotion she'd felt because of Johnny's music, and maybe because she'd discovered that she loved him, had dissipated somewhat by meeting her father.

Sitting, she closed her eyes and willed herself back into that practice room, back into that Rachmaninoff concerto. As she heard the notes again, her heart, chest, throat swelled with renewed passion.

She took her paint brush, squeezed a few colors on her palette, started to place the color on a canvas. Totally lost in the moment, she worked until she felt exhaustion set in. Then she stepped back to see what had come from her subconscious. That was where the good work was hidden, she realized. If she tried to force a picture, tried to reason it out, it was flat and amateurish. When she gave over, dug deep, let go, she got a picture that was worthwhile. That pleased her to learn that. Learning about the place from which a painting came was a giant step forward for her work.

She was flying. In the picture she was flying. She laughed out loud. Long plumes of scarlet and purple and blue covered her body, but elongated arms pointed across the sky. Long legs with bare feet trailed. Flames from the ground licked towards her. Thunderous gray clouds threatened on her left. She flew towards a bright light coming from the right side of the picture. The source of the light was hidden. That didn't matter. There's where the viewer would use his or her imagination. What was the source of the light she flew towards so eagerly?

"It's uplifting without being frivolous. Good work, LaDonna." His praise made her feel like flying. "Is flying always so hazardous for you?" His voice was deep, his laughter rumbling deeper.

She sighed and started cleaning up her brushes. "Sometimes just living seems awfully hazardous, Mr. Sable."

"You're thinking of the girl who was murdered, aren't you?"

"You know about that?"

"I heard."

"Do—do you know who did it? I mean, if you can—" How to put this. Did this—this—ghost wander all over the campus, coming here when she did, but otherwise have the ability to be anyplace he liked. "Do you go to other buildings whenever you feel like it?"

"Would you like to see my studio?"

"You work—you paint down here? Or near here?" This situation moved beyond her imagination, so all she could do was say yes and see what happened next. Before he could answer, she continued. "I'd love to see your studio."

"Come."

She still could not see this man who kept her company in the basement room, but when the door opposite the door to the upper floors opened, she stepped that way.

Again, she was assailed by musty air, air which had probably been trapped here for a long time.

"I can't see." The light from the basement reached only a few feet into the darkness.

"Follow my footsteps."

She swallowed, straightened her shoulders, and took several steps forward. Then she continued, guided only by the rustle and soft thud of his feet ahead of her.

Her father had told her once of the tunnels that ran underneath all the campus buildings. The metal tubes held pipes, underground power lines, air ducts. In some places this tunnel was large enough to stand upright, in others she had to bend over slightly to continue behind him. Mr. Sable warned her when this was the case, and she let her hand reach up and guide her.

Cobwebs brushed against her fingers, causing her to jerk back. Dust floated in the air, probably raised by their—her— feet. How long since anyone had walked here?

The thick ebony air began to make her feel trapped. She had no idea where she was walking, how to get back unless he guided her. When she could no longer touch the ceiling, she stretched her arms ahead, swimming in inky blackness that got colder the farther she walked.

She shivered, wishing she had worn her jacket. She had never liked caves and was easily claustrophobic. The feeling of being smothered wrapped round her.

"Is—is it much farther?"

"Trust me." His voice came from directly ahead of her.

She was. She realized she had placed a lot of trust, maybe her life in this man's hands, and she didn't even know who he was, what he was.

Just as she thought she might start screaming, they stopped. She heard the click of a lock, the twist of a doorknob. Paint smells, a touch of the familiar, soothed her nerves.

Then a dim light came on. The cord dangled in the center of the room as if a soft breeze had touched it. She began to see around her. The small room was piled with art supplies, covered with dust. The brushes, the paint tubes hadn't been touched for years. The walls were covered with more of his work, and for a few minutes she stood, turning to the next, the next, and the next painting, admiring them all. The style was easily recognizable, the work all fierce, angry, sorrowful, mystical, or sad. She felt as if the walls were papered with raw emotion.

A few sculptures posed in various

stages of completeness. Only two seemed finished.

"You worked in clay?" She felt he was still there with her.

"I tried. I gave it up. I couldn't express myself with that media. But this was my best attempt."

For just a few seconds she thought she was going to be able to see her companion. His fingers materialized near a stallion that reared, hooves pawing musty air.

The hands she saw reminded her of Johnny's. Long, slim fingers, strong fingers, an artist's fingers, the fingers of a sculptor, even though he admitted he had given that up.

The hands faded.

"Oh, for a moment—why won't you let me see you?"

"It's not necessary." His voice—was he angry with her? Or disappointed? She couldn't quite make out what he was feeling.

"It's all right," she quickly assured him. "I don't mind, really, I don't."

"You are a rare individual, LaDonna. Most people would have been afraid of me."

"Should I be?"

"Of course not. But they would not have believed, or they would have demanded more."

"You would have known that. You would never have spoken to them."

"That's right. I knew I could speak to you. I needed to speak to you. Thank you, LaDonna."

"I should thank you. You've given me back my art, my talent."

"Your talent never left you. It was your confidence that left. It took only your working again to restore it."

All the time they talked, she studied his work. Fell in love with every piece. Wanted to take them all back to the basement gallery. Then show them to—to the world.

"Has anyone else ever seen these paintings, Mr. Sable?"

There was a long moment of silence. But he hadn't gone. He hadn't left her here alone.

"I didn't—I—"

He left then. He left her in the dim room, far back under the campus, alone.

"Mr. Sable? Mr. Sable, please come back. I'm sorry. I didn't mean to pry."

Begging, pleading was of no use. He was gone. She almost panicked. How could she find her way back to the art building basement? She couldn't even remember how far it was.

"Please show me the way back." Her voice sounded hollow, flat, and insignificant in this place.

She moved to the door and looked back the way they had come. She could see nothing but flat, black air. Her mind created a maze of tunnels that twisted and turned. A path that could lead to nowhere, or one she could wander for days without seeing the light.

But she couldn't stay here. She pulled the string on the overhead bulb that had lit the room dimly. Stepped into the river of darkness. Swam with only hope for her return to light.

She forced herself to walk slowly, but with purpose. She pretended she knew the way, had walked it for a million nights. The darkness was nothing to fear.

Her hands made fists. Her stomach tightened. Her breathing became labored, heavy desperate sucking. She calmed herself. In and out, in and out. Deeply. There was plenty of air, stale, but life giving. In and out, in and out. Step by step. Step by step. Forward. There were no wrong turns. There was only the one pathway back. He would not let her lose her way.

She did trust him.

She entertained herself with questions. She had almost seen him. Why hadn't he let her see his face? Was he deformed? Scarred? The man without a face? She thought of that story, that book. The film. "It doesn't matter," she whispered.

A sudden impulse to run flooded over her. No. No, I will not run. If I run, I will lose my way. I will run into something. She kept her hands stretched in front of her and sometimes moved them to the side or overhead. She touched nothing.

She breathed a sigh of relief when she spotted dim light ahead. Her steps quickened. Reaching the basement room, she slipped in, closed the door firmly behind her. She widened her eyes and stared at her own studio, since that was what this room was becoming. She had done little work on sorting the donated paintings since she had started painting. But she had turned in no hours. She would be honest about her time here.

Would they let her stay if she wasn't working? She hadn't thought of that. Tomorrow she would return and dig into more of the boxes stacked against the walls. She would divide her time between her work and the college's work.

She could never leave this place now that he had shared his secret with her.

"Thank you," she whispered again. "I won't tell anyone unless you give me permission."

He hadn't asked her to make that promise, but somehow, she felt she must. He had done so much for her. Restored her work. And now, somehow restored her ability to walk through the darkness with confidence. Was that why he had left her?

How many more tests would he expect her to pass?

eleven

THE NEXT DAY at school, LaDonna had two new paintings to share. The one of Johnny, who no one knew was Johnny except her. And the one of her flying. She stood studying all three pieces of new work when Roddy stopped beside her.

He looked at the paintings for a long time. For so long that LaDonna started to worry.

"You don't like them, do you?" she asked.

"On the contrary, I'm rather impressed." Roddy smiled at her. "I want you to enter the district art competition for high school students."

"I don't know if I want to. I'll have to think about it. And I'll ask my—" She started to say teacher, but she didn't want to hurt Roddy's feelings. He had worked with her for three years without helping her this much. "—my dad." She finished the sentence.

"Are you working with someone, La-Donna?" Roddy asked.

"No one—you'd know." No one you'd believe is what she really meant.

"Try me. I know most of the artists in this area."

"I'd rather not say, Roddy. Maybe another time."

Roddy nodded and left her still looking at her work. She prepared another canvas board, then stood staring at it. She couldn't even make her hand reach up and start to draw.

"Where are you getting those paintings, LaDonna?" Eric Hunter asked, making her jump. He had sneaked up behind her.

"Don't sneak up behind me like that," she said. Eric had sounded angry and she answered with anger of her own.

"I didn't sneak up. I've been standing here and you didn't know it. I don't think you painted those. I see you hesitating, looking at your canvas now. You haven't put anything on a picture except gesso since I came into this art class."

"That doesn't mean I can't paint at home. And it's none of your business anyway, whether or not I painted these three pictures. Roddy doesn't doubt me."

"Roderiquez is too soft on you kids. Especially you. When I was in high school we called people like you teacher's pet. I guess things haven't changed much. Luis believes everything you tell him."

"That's because he knows I wouldn't lie to him." LaDonna turned her back to Eric, indicating that their conversation was finished.

She tried to let go of the anger he had caused her to feel. And to be honest, the doubt. She still had the lingering doubt, the idea that Mr. Sable had painted these pictures, using her hand.

She had read about automatic writing. A spirit comes into a person and guides his hand, writes a story through the medium. If a spirit could write like that, why not paint like that? She chewed her lip and wished she could paint something similar to her pictures now. Then she'd know the work was hers.

Hunter moved over to pester Johnny. Johnny had come to school today, but he had been awfully quiet. In today's class, he had moved away from everyone and had painted with his back to the class over in one corner. Eric Hunter interrupted his solitude, not even considering that it might be rude. If Eric planned to be a sensitive teacher that kids would respect, he had a long way to go and a lot to learn.

It was no use. LaDonna gave up on

painting in class. Maybe she could eventually, but not today. She'd let the canvas board dry, take it to work tomorrow. She didn't plan to try another painting in the basement gallery anyway. She needed to put in some hours on the real work she was hired to do.

As she washed her brushes, she glanced from the sink into Roddy's office. One corner of the room had been inclosed with half walls and glass windows. Roddy could take a student in there and talk to him, yet keep his eyes on the rest of the class. The door was seldom closed. But it was today.

And that wasn't all that attracted LaDonna's attention. The whole class had noticed. There was a policeman in the office talking to Roddy. Roddy was shaking his head, but LaDonna couldn't hear what he was saying.

She shouldn't stare. Quickly she shook the water from the fist full of brushes, grabbed a paper towel to soak up the rest of the water in them.

Since Johnny appeared to be finished for the day, she approached him. His face, still turned from the class, was stormy.

"Johnny? Want to talk?"

"Why do they have to come up here?"

"The police?"

"Wasn't it enough for them to question me at home and at Old Main? Now the whole school will be talking. The police think I killed Katherine, LaDonna. I'm sure they do."

"They can't possibly think that, Johnny." LaDonna felt a stab of sympathy along with disbelief.

"They can think anything they like."

"I think they questioned my father several times. Just because he cleans up there." She didn't mention the incident in the hall when she slipped out of Johnny's practice room. "They're going to keep talking to anyone who was anywhere near Old Main the night of the murder. It's routine. You have to ignore them."

"Maybe you're right."

"I think maybe we should play hooky from art and music and go to a movie after school. How does that grab you?"

"I need to practice. The recitals aren't that far away."

"And Roddy wants me to enter the district art competition. But I'd say we're too stressed to do anything well tonight."

"Okay, let's go all out. We'll stop at the house and make popcorn. I'll get Mom's car. We'll make it a real date." The anger left his eyes as he looked at LaDonna. She liked what she saw there in place of it. The softness, the—the—yes, love for her in Johnny's eyes made her feel all soft inside.

Roddy stopped them on the way out.

"LaDonna, are you still working at the art building on campus at night?"

"Sure. Thanks, that was a perfect job for me. I'm seeing so much bad art, mine seems halfway professional."

"That's good. But maybe you should just work afternoons. I'm worried about your being up there at night."

"Has something else happened?" She hadn't looked at a newspaper for days.

Roddy hesitated. "I guess you'll read it in the newspaper soon enough. Another young woman was assaulted last night, late. She got away, but she was darned scared. She didn't get a look at the man who jumped her, but he tried to strangle her. All she could say was that he had long, slender fingers. Strong fingers. And that he seemed really angry."

LaDonna shivered without meaning to. Maybe it was foolish for her to walk across the campus late at night. But a strange thought came into her mind.

I don't have to worry. He'll protect me.

twelve

WHEN THEY CAME out of the school, La-Donna would have fainted if she hadn't had hold of Johnny's arm. His mother waited in the parking lot. She honked and waved to get their attention.

"Your mother?" LaDonna said, looking at Johnny. "Why isn't she at work?" Then a flash of fear hit her. "Something must be wrong." She pulled a reluctant Johnny over to the car. "Mrs. Blair, what's wrong?"

"Are you all right, Mom?" Johnny finally spoke.

"Yes, yes, yes, and nothing is wrong, but I didn't want you two to go up on the campus today. Get in. I'll take you home."

"Mom." Johnny was embarrassed. "You're being silly."

"We were both going to cut work and go to the movies." LaDonna felt disappointment now that she found Johnny's mom was just doing her Super-mom act. She had been looking forward to some down time with Johnny.

"You can go later. Come on, Johnny. Get in."

Johnny sighed, shrugged, and opened the front passenger door for LaDonna. Then he got in the back of their old Subaru.

"I don't want you or LaDonna on that campus today, Johnny. You can practice at home." Mrs. Blair headed toward home.

"Mother, I can't stop practicing on the grand. I have a recital in May and I'm nowhere near ready."

"And I can't quit my job," LaDonna added. "I need the money." No one, *nothing* was going to make her stop going to the basement room.

"Another girl was assaulted up there last night, LaDonna. She got away, but it could have just as easily have been you. That campus is not safe. Your boss will understand. Tell him you'll come back after they catch this maniac."

"Mom, how did you find that out?" Johnny asked. "It hasn't been in the papers."

"We hear everything at the store. Some students came in later and told us the whole story. They had gathered around when the girl got away and called the police."

LaDonna turned and looked at Johnny. He was staring out the window. His hands lay in his lap. She stared at his long, slender fingers. Strong fingers.

How silly. She forced her eyes to move to his long bony face and she missed his crooked smile. It had been days since Johnny had smiled.

"Take me home, Mrs. Blair. We can still make the five-thirty movie, Johnny. Okay?"

"Sure. Be there in a little while." Johnny held the door open for LaDonna. He looked upset. She ran inside, leaving him to deal with his mother.

Her father hadn't left for work, and she didn't ask why. When she walked into the kitchen he was eating a TV dinner. He glanced up but didn't say anything. My happy family, thought LaDonna. She hurried into her room to change clothes. She would wear her best jeans, and a new sweatshirt.

Thinking of something she wanted to ask her dad, she hurried back to the kitchen. He was sipping a cup of coffee.

"Dad, I've heard that there are tunnels under all the buildings on campus. Is that right?" She'd pretend she knew nothing.

"Sure. They're air ducts. They hold

pipes and electrical systems. Phone lines. Some are closed off, but you can get through most of them. Why do you ask?"

"Just curious. The idea fascinates me. I wonder if anyone could live down there?"

Her father studied his coffee. His fingers circled the mug where cream clouded the dark liquid. The fingers on his right hand were stained yellow with nicotine. The doctor had told him to stop smoking but he probably never would. He just didn't smoke at home any more. Permanent dirt and grime emphasized the lines and his fingernails. She had never noticed how long her father's fingers were. She was sure they were strong. He had used them for hard work all his life.

Finally he answered her question. "I guess so. But I've never heard of it. The transients stay on the streets to pick up spare change and sleep in the park or occasionally the homeless shelter if they can get out there. Most of the tunnels are locked since they have outlets into the buildings and the buildings are locked."

"Johnny Blair and I are going to the early movie." She jumped up and completely changed the subject so her father wouldn't think about her question for too long. "I'd better get some popcorn made."

"I heard about a guy who got arrested for taking his own popcorn to the movies."

"We're sneaky. We can barely afford the movie, much less the refreshments."

"You need some money?" Her father reached in the pocket of his overalls.

"No, Dad, really. I'm working now, remember?"

"Maybe you shouldn't go up on the campus for awhile." If he hadn't remembered before, he did now.

"I'll be all right. I'm careful." She ran back to her room to unbraid her hair and brush it. She didn't need another lecture.

There were four movies showing at the dollar seventy-five theater, the only one she ever went to. Six or seven dollars for a movie just wasn't in her budget, and she never expected Johnny to buy her ticket. When they went someplace together, it was never like a date. Until now, she had never considered they were any more than friends. She wasn't sure she liked thinking anything else. It might ruin their friendship.

They chose the scary movie, of course. And they weren't disappointed. This woman kept running around inside and out of a big apartment building in New York City. And she just happened to have rented the apartment where another woman had killed herself—jumped out the window. But you knew she didn't jump. If she had, there wouldn't have been a story.

Some weirdo was watching her all the time, since he'd put a hidden camera in her apartment. How come he hadn't seen the former tenant jump out the window? Or be pushed? Unless he was the murderer, too.

"Da-da, da-da. Da-da, da-da." Johnny hummed the Jaws theme as they left the movie. "Want to live in New York City some day?" He laughed.

"I don't think so. Fortunately artists can live anyplace."

"So can pianists. But I'll have to travel a lot. So I guess it won't matter where I live. I'll just have one room and a piano."

"With a cheap, cozy little restaurant down the block so you don't have to cook. Can you cook?"

"Is this a proposal?" Johnny teased.

"Well, I can't cook. Someone has to."

"There are always TV dinners."

LaDonna remembered her father's dinner. And sometimes you eat them when neither you or your daughter wants to cook.

"Did you hear about that girl being attacked when you came across campus last night, Johnny?" LaDonna moved back to the subject uppermost on her mind. Maybe they should have seen a light comedy at the theater.

"Is that a subtle way of asking me if I was up there?"

"You're really sensitive about that, aren't you?"

"You would be too if the police kept asking you questions. Why would I kill Katherine?"

LaDonna made an attempt at black humor. "She was a better pianist than you?"

Johnny sighed. He hadn't told a dark, tasteless joke for weeks. "That's not funny."

"I know. I'm sorry. We'll talk about something else."

They got very quiet for three blocks. Three dark blocks along Broadway and onto The Hill.

LaDonna laughed a little. "We're brilliant conversationalists, aren't we?"

"Your new art says a lot. Want to tell me why you're painting with that new style?"

"No. Did you notice that one of them is you? And that another is how I felt after I listened to your music the other day."

"When you slipped out quietly."

"You heard me."

"No. But when I finished playing, I asked you if you were bored. You weren't. You were gone. I was playing for you."

"I'm sorry. I appreciated it. But suddenly—well, it's hard to explain. I was so filled with emotion from listening, I thought I was going to burst. I just had to paint. I'm painting in the basement, on the job. But I don't charge off those hours."

"I suspected you were. What's there that makes you able to paint when you can't paint in class? Or at home?"

"Have you forgotten that I told you someone was there with me?" If he had forgotten, she'd remind him. She needed to talk about Mr. Sable again.

"You still believe that? To tell the truth, LaDonna, I didn't pay much attention to you when you told me that the first time. That's your imagination."

"No!" Wow, she didn't mean to be that adamant. In a quieter voice she said, "No, it's not my imagination. He's helping me paint. My style's a lot like his, but I've stopped worrying about that. I can't explain it, Johnny. It's like he—he gets inside my mind and guides my hand."

"Then it's his painting."

"No, I refuse to believe that. My emotion is reflected in the work."

They walked a ways farther. "Should I worry about you, LaDonna? Are you losing your mind? Why don't you talk to the counselor at the school? She's pretty good. I went to see her last year when I had trouble with my scheduling."

"I don't need a psychiatrist or a psychologist. I do need a friend, Johnny. Believe what I'm telling you."

"It's hard." He draped his arm around her loosely. "You're telling me you believe in ghosts. I don't. So we don't have a meeting of minds. Like—like you say you do with this—this person in your basement room. You were awfully stressed, LaDonna, when—"

"Why did I tell you?" LaDonna felt slightly hurt that Johnny couldn't understand what she was telling him. But if she thought about it for long, she could see his point. If he told her he was playing music that someone else put in his head, not off a page in a book, but coming to him through the air, would she believe him? Or would she say, you've lost your mind, Johnny.

"Because we've always shared everything." He hugged her. "Don't stop sharing just because I think you're weird." He pushed her and ran ahead. She chased him to the corner. Then they both had to stop for a traffic light.

After a couple more blocks they were passing the north end of the campus. "Want to go practice, Johnny?" she asked. "I can walk on home by myself."

"Your dad and my mother would kill me."

"They would never know. But I guess I'll try to paint at home tonight. That's the worst of this situation, Johnny, whatever it is. I'm starting to feel as if I can't paint any place except in that musty basement. If that's the case, I'm in trouble."

"I heard that's called functional fixedness. A big word for being rigid. Only being able to do whatever it is you do in one place. I'll practice at home tonight. You paint in your room. Willing to try?"

"Deal." LaDonna stuck out her hand and shook Johnny's. And when they reached her house, she knew their evening had ended with that handshake. She would rather have had a kiss.

thirteen

After two nights of unsuccessfully trying to paint at home, LaDonna slipped out after her father left for work and hurried to the campus. Her father had not forbidden her to go to her job, but he had strongly suggested that it wasn't a good idea. Roddy had said the same thing. Johnny hadn't bothered. He knew she'd do as she pleased.

She figured she could always catch up on sorting the donated paintings, but now that she was working well, she hated to let her painting go. Facing a blank canvas was scary enough. Facing one, knowing you were blocked was hell.

She didn't know what it was like to be pregnant, but she could imagine how frustrating it must be to want to have your baby and not be able to. When she wanted to paint and couldn't, it was as if she had this huge living thing inside her trying to get out. The more it pushed and kicked, the more miserable she felt. And the less she wanted to live through the pain.

Spring had returned after the snow squall and the night was damp, smelling of hyacinths, and buds were bursting from all the trees.

But the night was also moonless. As she entered the campus from College Avenue, she realized that the lights on either side of Varsity Pond were either burned out or had been broken.

Her feet thudded on the walk as she walked faster and faster. All the warnings from adults around her had made her nervous. She hated the feeling. She hated being afraid.

"LaDonna, wait." A low whisper escaped the grove of pines to her left. "La-Donna, what's your hurry?"

She stopped, glanced around, but could see nothing but dark, straight tree trunks against an even darker background.

For a couple of seconds she thought the voice belonged to Mr. Sable, but what would he be doing out here?

"Who's there?" she said, angry because her voice was tentative.

She stepped onto the bridge, grasped

the cold wall to the left of the walk, leaned slightly over. A light on the other side of the pond reflected in the shiny water as if that was where the moon had tried to hide.

Trip-trap, trip-trap. She continued to walk, remembering the story now. The troll was at the other end.

Why had the fairy tale come to mind? Because in third grade she had played the Biggest Billy Goat Gruff, the one who was supposed to deal with the troll. She had been as fearless in third grade as she had until—until just a few weeks ago. The other kids had known that when they chose her for the part.

Trip-trap. She hurried on. *Trip-trap.* She ran.

His laughter followed her. She wanted to go back and fight. He had deliberately tried to frighten her. And he had succeeded.

Who? Someone who knew her. Someone who had followed her all this way from home? Or someone who knew she wouldn't be able to stay home and work for long?

That could be half a dozen people. Johnny, Luis Rodriguez, Eric Hunter, her father, Mr. Sable.

Or even her boss, Glen Walker. She didn't see much of him, but when she did, he waved. And he knew she liked to work at night. Maybe he wasn't the nice guy Roddy thought he was. Something could have happened to push him over the edge. Many people today, due to stress and unhappiness or anger, walked a fine line between being a nice person and one out of control, taking their anger out on society.

Was this person's scaring her tonight separate from what was happening on campus, or—or was he ...

She couldn't think of any reason for anyone *she* knew to be attacking women at night. But suddenly she knew some very strange people. Why had Mr. Sable selected her to appear to in the basement gallery? He could be in her imagination, she realized, but she didn't think so. Someone speaking to her on the bridge wasn't made up, was it?

Her life had certainly taken a strange turn.

Artists, very creative people, walked a narrow line between sanity and a disturbed personality. Maybe ... Wow, now she was thinking she was going crazy.

She had to use her key to get into the art building. The lock was stubborn. Twice she glanced around while she jiggled and twisted it. This outside light burned brightly. She saw no one, and there were no close bushes for anyone to hide.

Hurrying through the dimly lighted hall, she reached the stairway door. She stopped, listened. She had never come into the building this late at night, alone, she realized. She usually came in by day, when people were having classes in the building. Often she left at night, but entering the place at night felt strange. Sometimes there were night classes. Not tonight.

She thought she'd feel safe when she reached her room. She didn't. Her hands shook as she got out her brushes and paints. As she squeezed color on her palette.

Paint from your emotion. She would. She had plenty tonight. She would paint from her fear.

She piled blue and gray in layers at the bottom left of the canvas like icebergs, waiting, watching. A night sky of ebony. A lop-sided, waning moon, as cold as the ice below.

From a navy-colored ocean, a killer whale breached, his body slick with trailing drops of water, the surface breaking into teardrops of clear crystal. The whale's body, black patterned with white, matched the landscape, but his energy, his powerful leap from the ocean depths suggested a contrast.

He would glow, glow with phosphorescence. She searched for cad yellow light, squeezed out a worm of paint, drew it lightly around the whale's body. A hint of green. A dry brush dragged still another cool color across the yellow.

"What are you afraid of?" the smooth voice said, drifting from the shadowed corner behind her.

"Oh!" She jumped and dropped her paint brush. She bent to pick it up and felt foolish. "I didn't know you were here." She wiped paint from the floor.

"Your concentration, your focus was excellent. Perhaps I shouldn't have disturbed you. Frightened you."

"I'm almost finished. I guess I'm still jumpy from someone following me on the way over here." She'd tell him. See what he said.

"You're alone in the building."

Thanks—I guess, she thought.

"You're welcome."

He could read her mind.

"That surprises you?"

"Hey, stop it." She tried to smile and turned back to the painting.

The moon radiates with the same colors, the same green and yellow glow.

"Echoing the algae on the whale," she whispered.

Perhaps the wall of ice on the left

"would reflect the glow." She dragged some yellow and a touch of green paint along the iceberg.

127

And below, under the water, in the ocean depths

"a hint of blue,"

and gray,

"just like the ice, as if he burst from ice way down, from the depths of icy darkness, the unknown."

Silence surrounded them. She studied the picture. Decided it was finished and that she liked it. The style was a bit more realistic than her others, but the mix of colors set it apart, kept it from being just another nature picture.

She remembered the title of a book she'd seen while passing a bookstore window. *The Moon by Whale Light*. Maybe that idea stayed in her mind. Could she call her painting by the same name? The idea, the image fit perfectly.

She didn't know how long she had sat there, pulled into the cold, arctic glow, but at about the same time she started to shiver, a sharp sound startled her.

Even through the thick brick walls of the old building, she heard the siren shriek through the night. The wail seemed to stop very close to where she worked.

fourteen

QUICKLY SHE CLEANED up, but found then she was afraid to leave the building. Funny that she felt more comfortable—safer—in this musty basement room with someone— a ghost she'd have to call him—here with her, than she did out in the real world.

But knowing what had been happening on campus combined with the siren so close caused an apprehension that froze her blood and numbed her legs.

Finally she stood. She climbed the stairs, walked down the empty hall, leaned on the front door to open it. As soon as she turned right and rounded the corner of the art building, she raised her hand to shield her eyes. The area around Varsity Pond was lit up as if a fraternity was holding a rock concert there.

There was no concert.

A crowd had gathered. Slowly she walked up behind some students. "Do you know what's happening?"

The story had circulated fast. "They're dragging the pond."

"It takes two days to drain it."

"Who—what are they looking for?" La-Donna asked.

"Someone reported a scream, some cries, and a splash."

"They're afraid another girl has been killed."

Several people helped tell the story. La-Donna didn't add her share. She didn't say, *that could be me they're looking for. I think he followed me earlier.*

Should she find a policeman and tell him she thought someone was looking for a victim around eight o'clock? She didn't know that. She didn't see him. No, she wouldn't talk to the police. She had no real evidence.

She walked back to the sidewalk just west of the art building and cut downhill to College Avenue, watching as policemen searched the woods with their spotlights.

Under a street lamp she glanced at her watch. It was eleven. The streets were almost empty, except for an occasional car. No one was walking.

Hurrying from light to light, she stayed alert, ready to run at any noise. *He has already killed tonight. He has no need to kill again.*

Where did that idea come from? She didn't know. It seemed logical. For the first time in a long time, she wished she had a close girl friend. Someone she could call when she got home to an empty house and needed to talk. Just to share ideas. Maybe someone to share the idea that it had almost been her tonight, that she was playing with fire to keep going onto campus alone after dark.

Lights were still on at Johnny's house. She knew his mother liked to stay up late. Mrs. Blair had trouble sleeping. Did La-Donna dare ring the bell?

She did. She pushed it, hoping Johnny would answer. He stayed up late, too.

Mrs. Blair peeked out, then opened the door. "LaDonna, what are you doing out here so late?"

"Is Johnny home? Or asleep. I just needed to talk to him."

"He's in the shower. He hasn't been home long, but he came right in and headed for the bathroom. I expect he'll come back downstairs before he goes to bed. He usually stops and talks to me for a minute. It's the only time we have together most days."

What Mrs. Blair was really saying was, go home, LaDonna. Johnny is mine now. I don't want to share him.

"Well, okay, I'd better go. Tell him I said hi and that I'll talk to him tomorrow."

"I'll do that, LaDonna. Now you hurry home, you hear? You shouldn't be out here so late by yourself. You didn't come off the campus, did you? I just watched the news. I don't even like for Johnny to be up there."

LaDonna wasn't going to share anything with Mrs. Blair. "I'll run. Don't worry about me."

She did run after looking up and down the sidewalk in front of the Blairs. At her own door, she hurriedly pushed the key into the lock and twisted, jumped inside and slammed the door. Leaned against it.

Johnny just came home? And went straight to the shower? Would someone who just murdered a girl be covered with blood? It might depend on how he killed her. Strangling someone wouldn't cause the killer to get bloody. Stabbing her would. Especially if she fought, as Katherine had.

Without wanting to, LaDonna pictured Johnny's long, strong fingers on black and white piano keys. She felt his hand in hers. His hand at her waist, long fingers pressing in slightly to pull her close for a hug or to keep them together walking with his arm around her.

Johnny could not kill anyone, she said

over and over to herself as she headed for a shower. Are you sure? that other self said, as if it was a part of her.

I'm not sure of anything anymore.

She showered, slipped into an old soft nightgown, and lay on her bed. She stared at the faded wallpaper, the cracks in the ceiling that she had made into animals and plants when she was very young.

She snapped off the light. Lay in the soft darkness for what seemed like hours. Nothing made sense to her since Mr. Sable had come into her life. What did that mean? Nothing really. And one thing was right. Her work.

She felt good about tonight's painting.

fifteen

THERE WAS NO way LaDonna could avoid reading the headlines in the newspaper the next morning.

CAMPUS KILLER STRIKES AGAIN

Her dad studied the front page while he sipped his coffee. The smell made La-Donna nauseous. She'd be lucky to keep down tea and toast.

When her father handed her the front page of the paper, she debated whether or not she wanted to read the article. Curiosity won. Someone would tell her anyway.

Teachers said that Minette Waterson was the most promising young artist they'd seen for years. Waterson stayed on campus late last night to finish hanging her senior show, a show that will now hang as a memorial to this young woman.

Around ten o'clock police were called to Varsity Pond by women from the nearby sorority house. One of them had heard screams, what sounded like a fight, and then a splash. Another witness said he saw someone running in the direction of College Avenue right after ten.

It took police less than an hour to locate Waterson's body. Speculation is that she was dead before she hit the water, however. There were numerous knife wounds on her body, one of which was probably fatal.

Retracing Waterson's steps before she reached the pond, led back to the art room where she had spent the evening. The young artist's work is nothing short of spectacular.

The police are continuing their investigation. Anyone with further information or who was in the vicinity of Varsity Pond last night is asked to come in and talk with authorities.

LaDonna stared at the newsprint, which blurred before her eyes. I spoke with her. She had my job. She was in the basement. I should go in, she thought over and over. I know I should. And would they get it out of me that Johnny got home about ten thirty? That he immediately went to shower? That someone who knew me

135

called my name earlier? Someone tried to frighten me. Guilt battled with fear.

Another list of police questions filled her mind. Where did you go after someone tried to frighten you? Why didn't you call us then? If she said she went to paint, they might ask to see her painting, or where she was painting. Then they might ask if she went straight home at eleven o'clock. She could say yes. There was no one at her house to say she didn't.

This was all too complicated.

"LaDonna are you all right?" Her dad stared at her.

"Yes, Dad. Thanks. I guess with as many people as there are on campus, a couple are certain to be—be—" LaDonna wasn't sure what to call someone who would murder women for no reason, or none that anyone could see.

"Crazy." Her dad finished the sentence. "This killer is psychotic. He probably acts perfectly natural most of the time."

Her dad seemed so sure about his statement, but LaDonna agreed. Again she realized the killer could be someone she knew. *He called your name.* "Someone called my name."

"What? Someone called you last night?" Her father seemed interested.

"Oh, no, I was just thinking out loud. It was nothing, Dad, nothing."

She put her cup in the sink and dashed out of the house.

Johnny wasn't at school. She missed him. And what did that mean? Was he sick? Hiding out?

She messed with a canvas in art class. Mr. Rodriguez ignored her, giving a lot of attention to Merilee. Eric Hunter spent the class setting up a still life and helping three girls do charcoal sketches. LaDonna had the strange feeling that she was invisible.

She tried to think invisible was good right now. Her instinct told her to lie low. Not volunteer information that could be twisted and turned against Johnny, or anyone else. She hurried up to the college campus after school. She had changed her mind about going straight to work. She wanted to see the senior show the young woman who was killed had stayed late hanging. There might be something in her work that would tell LaDonna more about her. She felt as if she really wanted to know Minette Waterson.

Another building held the art labs where most of the actual painting, sculpting, iron work, crafts was done. LaDonna hurried past her classroom building and into the long hall of the next where paint, glue, wood, and clay smells mixed into a heavenly aroma—if you were an artist.

LaDonna was reminded of the smell of newly sharpened pencils, her new paint box, the new book smells of first grade.

She passed a display of batik and stopped to look at the work, stalling, she knew, but she let it be all right.

Last year she had been obsessed by silk screen, but now she knew fine art would be her major in college. Painting. She could never make a living with it, at least not right away, but she'd work someplace in order to paint. Roddy was trying to get her a scholarship in art. Maybe Minette Waterson was here on an art scholarship. Was that why she had first accepted the job from Glen? Was her spectacular art salable? LaDonna would compare it to what she was doing. What would four more years of experience help her to produce?

Go in the gallery, LaDonna. Go in and see her paintings. Somehow LaDonna had equated seeing Minette's art to seeing her body at a funeral service. She took a deep breath, swallowed, and pulled open the door to the student gallery.

The place was jammed with people. That didn't surprise LaDonna. Curiosity seekers. People with a morbid sense of needing to see. Did she fall into that category?

Did it matter why she was here?

Spectacular was the right word for the

reporter to have used. Incredible, terrific—
all those superlatives. Tears came to La-
Donna's eyes that hadn't been there before. Within a few minutes Minette
returned to life through her work. What
a wasted talent.

Like Katherine. Was that the key to the
killer's victims? Women who were incredibly talented? The woman who got away
was a dancer. Or was that a coincidence?
Those students would work long hours,
creating or practicing.

She was staring at a long, narrow canvas picturing a young man, a man with an
elongated body, long, slender hands that
reached for the sky. The piece was entitled
"Desire." LaDonna understood the emotion. The reaching for, the longing for
something.

"God, she had talent, didn't she?" said
a deep voice behind her. "Like you do."

LaDonna swung around to find Eric
Hunter right behind her, standing way too
close. She stepped away.

"Yes, she did." What else could she
say? What are you doing here? He was
doing the same thing LaDonna was, looking at the young artist's show.

"What a waste of talent," LaDonna
commented.

They stood side by side studying the
painting, and LaDonna felt Eric relax a little. His attitude helped her breathe more

normally, and before she could stop she sighed deeply.

"LaDonna, I owe you an apology." Eric said without looking at her. "I realize that every time we've talked I've rubbed you wrong. I'll even admit to having an abrasive personality."

"You will?" LaDonna smiled without looking at him.

"If you want to know the whole truth, I was scared that first day I came to class. Teenagers can be very intimidating."

"We always give student teachers a bad time. Same as substitute teachers."

"I know. I remember. I'm not that old."

Their silence was companionable as they moved to another painting, which surprised LaDonna. Finally Eric said, "Have a pizza or a sub with me? I'm sure you're heading for work, but you have to eat sometime. Give me a second chance?"

"How about mixing with your students?" she teased, giving her a few seconds to decide how she felt about being with him.

"I'm sure it's safe, and totally kosher as well. I promise not to come on to you."

"I am hungry." LaDonna realized she was starved. She'd had no breakfast. School lunch was a disaster. She couldn't go to work without eating.

"Okay, new start." LaDonna decided and offered her hand to Eric. She still wasn't sure how she felt about him, but she was willing to give him another chance to be cool. She wouldn't mind talking to someone about Minette Waterson's show.

He grinned and squeezed her palm hard. Then pushed her through the crowd to an exit. "I wonder how many would have attended her show without the publicity, the sensationalism."

"I would hope a lot would have come. Real art lovers who would appreciate her talent."

Teresa's had a line, so they went on to The Sub Shop. LaDonna found a table after telling Eric what she wanted. Waiting gave her time to watch him, and to think about this change in his attitude. Was it real? Did she care? She was only going to have a sandwich with him. She'd like to know more about him.

He answered her first question as he unwrapped the paper from his sandwich. "I came here last summer from New Jersey. I thought I'd live with my aunt who's here, but she's pretty old and somewhat of a recluse. I sensed she didn't want me around."

"Did you come on to her like you did to me—our whole class?" LaDonna asked.

"Well, I wasn't afraid of her. I think she's used to being alone with four cats and her memories."

"So where are you living?"

"I found a cheap room on Thirteenth. I don't dare leave anything valuable there. It's a dump."

"How about your work? Where do you leave it?"

"I don't think anyone would want a picture I painted." Eric studied his ham and cheese. "I'm not very good. My uncle was an artist. A good one. His paintings are worth a lot now."

LaDonna heard the word "was" but didn't pry. "I think some people get caught up in the romance of being a painter." Quickly she added, "I don't mean you, but everyone. No one realizes how hard it is, what hell it is, if you want the truth. I'm miserable when I'm not painting. I'm miserable when my work is going badly. Work was going badly when you came to school." Her words weren't really an apology, but an explanation of how she'd acted when she met him, if he wanted one.

"And now it is?" He smiled. He was really cute when he dropped his Mr. Wonderful act. "Going well?"

"Yes."

"What changed it for you? Got you out of your block?"

Had Roddy told Eric she was blocked or had he added one and one to get frustration? "I—I don't think I can tell you. I mean it would sound too strange. Some-one helped me."

"Roddy?"

"No. Someone else. Roddy has helped me lots of times, but I was really down on myself this time. I needed more than words."

I needed someone whispering to me, leaning over my shoulder, showing me a path to explore.

"The work you brought in looked really familiar." Eric gave her space, but she could tell he was more than curious.

"I guess you could say someone influenced me a lot. But I've always studied the great artists. I really like the paintings Turner did late in life."

Eric stared at her until she felt uncomfortable with him again. She looked away and concentrated on her food. Her throat tightened around a piece of hard roll, so she reached for her Coke and sipped the sharp, fizzy drink, letting it slide down.

"Why don't you bring one of your paintings to class tomorrow, Eric?" La-Donna suggested. "Are you open to criticism?"

"By high school artists?"

"Oh, oh. There goes that chip back on your shoulder."

"You're really honest, aren't you?" He grinned at her.

"I don't lie to myself. And telling some-

143

one else his work is good when it isn't is of no use to him."

"Roddy said he often asked you to work with his beginning class. Have you thought of teaching?"

"Occasionally. Roddy is a good role model. You can learn a lot from him. Wow, I have to go to work. My dad has suggested strongly that I be home by dark."

"I don't blame him. Take the rest of your sub to work with you. What time do you get off? I could walk you home."

"Johnny usually does that." LaDonna wanted Eric to know she wasn't interested in him as a date, even if she had to lie a little. She wasn't even sure if Johnny was in the music rooms. And she never knew what time he'd finish.

"I thought you two were an item."

"We're friends." LaDonna put her leftovers in her bag and picked up her Coke.

"Speak of the devil and he appears." Eric grinned at someone behind her.

"LaDonna, I need to talk to you." Johnny Blair stepped up to their table.

"She has to go to work." Eric looked at LaDonna. A tiny smile, left from his grin, curled his lip down. He took on his spoiled, arrogant persona again.

"I'll walk her over there." Johnny put emphasis on the word I'll, as if to say, you leave her alone. Oh, my, was Johnny jealous? She hoped so.

"What are you doing with that guy?" Johnny said as soon as they left the shop.

"Why weren't you at school today?" LaDonna sparred with her own question.

"I wanted to stay home." For Johnny that was reason enough to do so. He always did as he pleased.

"You're in a blue funk, aren't you? Don't take it out on me." LaDonna recognized the depression that Johnny often dealt with. The emotion usually came on him when a recital got close. She knew it originated from his worry about being good enough.

Johnny didn't answer. He took her arm as they crossed a busy intersection on Broadway. His touch helped her feel a very mixed electrical charge between them.

Neither spoke until he delivered her to the growing shadows of trees near the front door of the art building. She didn't realize it was nearly five o'clock.

His firm grip on her arm stopped her, swung her around to face him. She looked up and tried to read the expression on his face, his eyes.

"I've started thinking of you as my girl, LaDonna." Johnny was as honest as she was, and she had to admit, she liked this

145

statement from him. But she stalled giving over to his mood.

"You don't own me."

"I didn't say that. I—I've realized that—" Johnny stopped squeezing her arm and looked away, towards Varsity Pond. "Oh, hell, LaDonna, I love you."

She laughed. "Is that so traumatic?"

He looked back into her eyes, and his gaze softened a little. "Yes, it is. I have a schedule for my life. I was going to fall in love about ten years from now." His shoulders slumped, and he finally laughed, too.

"You can love me, Johnny, and not do anything about it, except—except—"

"Except what?"

"Do I have to tell you what to do? You could kiss me." She tilted her lips to his. He didn't need any more encouragement.

His kiss was tender, then more passionate, and she responded until they were both breathless. She buried her face in his wooly flannel shirt, enjoying the smell of him, the warmth of his arms around her.

"I love you, too, Johnny," she said finally. "I realized that when I sat behind you the other night and heard you play, watched you practice. Let's make it all right. I have a lot of plans, too. We can love each other and not run away and get married, don't you think?"

"I hope so." He laughed again, took

146

both of her arms and pushed her away a little to look at her. "Would you please be careful? Or wait for me to come and get you tonight?"

"Was that what made you realize you loved me?"

"Partly. I don't want you—hurt."

"Please don't worry, Johnny. And don't think you have to worry about time in order to come get me. I can take care of myself," LaDonna assured him. She brushed his cheek with another kiss. "Bye."

I hope, she thought, as she ran towards her work. Knowing that Johnny loved her made her feel she could do anything.

sixteen

QUICKLY, SHE SORTED a box of paintings. To her surprise, there was one good one. She hung it on the wall to look at further. Finally, tired of unpacking boxes, she stared at a blank canvas waiting for her own work.

"Love is hard to paint," he said, his voice soft, sensual.

"You know?"

"I've known for a long time."

"Why didn't you tell me?"

"I knew he'd come around eventually. He's loved you for a long time without knowing it."

"He got scared when Katherine was killed."

"Are you still frightened?"

"Of you?"

"No, in general, of the darkness?"

She thought about that. "No," she said finally. "But someone is killing those women. I'm afraid of him. Do you know who the murderer is?"

"I haven't tried to find out."

"But you could. You can leave here?"

"I don't. I'm comfortable here."

So am I, thought LaDonna, realizing he'd read that thought.

She lost track of time, but spent a couple of hours in some kind of limbo, not painting, not thinking, just being. Finally she put her brushes, her tubes of paint away. Closed the box. Debated taking the whale painting to show Roddy. For some reason, she didn't want to share it yet. She left everything behind and climbed the stairs reluctantly. She hated to leave the soft quiet space, the cocoon where she felt accepted, fulfilled by her work, comfortable with him.

She stood in the glow of the street lamps and looked both ways. Walking by Varsity Pond frightened her. The path was tainted by images she didn't want to play through her mind. Going straight down the hill was shorter but the sidewalk entered a stretch of dark woods for about forty feet until it came out on College.

Don't think about it, she commanded her mind. Just hurry home. She turned left and hurried downhill.

Pines sighed in a soft breeze. She was surrounded by the smell of long, wet needles and cones that squirrels had nibbled into shreds, hunting the seeds.

He jumped her about the time she had relaxed and stopped worrying. Arms squeezed her from behind, steel bands that cut into her rib cage and forced air from her lungs. She had no voice to scream.

Struggling, she turned and twisted, kicked backwards with little force. He laughed, the sound low in her ear, his breath warm on her neck.

"Let me go!" she managed to say. Keep your wits, she told herself. He has to loosen his hold.

He picked her up, half carried, half dragged her into the deeper shadows. A soft carpet of pine needles muted her stomping and kicking.

The wet, slick ground cover helped her at last. She sagged, made her body dead weight in his arms. He slipped, and she took immediate advantage. Swinging around, kicking him as he fell, she half ran, half crawled until she could get to her feet. By then she had reached the sidewalk.

Confused, thinking only of escaping, she dashed back uphill onto the campus, heading for lights.

He was not that easily discouraged. In

seconds, she heard his feet thudding on the concrete behind her. Lungs aching, she doubled her efforts, gasping for air as she ran. Her mouth dried, which kept her from calling out. All she could manage was the panting and sucking of cool, moist air.

She had dropped the key to the art building into her jacket pocket earlier when she had let herself inside. Jamming her fist into the gaping denim flap, she grasped the slender metal. Her fingers closed over it, lifted it out, made sure the point was forward.

Throwing herself against the door, she slipped the key into the lock, twisted. She willed the lock not to stick, then flung the door wide. He grabbed it before she could turn and slam it shut.

Down the hall she raced. She banged the basement door open, thundered down the stairs, praying she wouldn't fall. She crossed the darkened gallery room and fled out the other door, knowing she had a tiny advantage here. She knew where she was.

She stopped running, quieting her steps. She knew he had followed her, but now he felt his way. Both of them were blanketed by darkness.

The air in the tunnel was stale, musty, but she sucked it in gratefully, and as quietly as possible. Slowly, slowly, she let the air fill her lungs, breathed it out even more slowly so no sound carried back to him.

Her arms held stiffly in front of her, she continued walking, moving as quickly as she dared. If she ran into something, he'd hear her. Follow her more easily. At this moment she had the advantage, since she knew they were in the tunnels. She knew the tunnel opened to rooms, to other buildings. If she could find one of those buildings, she could enter another building on campus, leave it and find help. A big if, since doors would probably be locked, and she would have no idea where she was. Also she would have to feel along the wall for an opening, taking precious time to search.

For a few seconds she considered pressing her back to one wall, staying there, letting him walk past her. Would that work? Or would he reach out and touch her, looking for a wall himself. Stopping was too risky. Stay ahead of him. That was the best plan. Worry about where she'd come out later.

Would he continue to follow her? Maybe he had already gone back. She stopped, listened. The softest of echoes reached her ears. Footsteps, tentative, shuffling. Not too close. Not far enough away. He was coming. Slowly. He was searching every bit of the space, looking for her.

Cobwebs brushed her outstretched fingers, sticky, soft. She jerked her hands back. Turned slightly. Cobwebs would be in a corner, wouldn't they? Would a tunnel have a corner? Okay, cobwebs would be closer to a wall. She wanted to stay in the center of the huge metal tubes.

Soon, walking in the darkness, she became confused, disoriented. She stumbled, caught herself before she fell, but gasped, and knew he would have heard the soft thud. She listened. Heard a soft thudding echo behind her. Of course he hadn't given up. He had her trapped. He would think.

The air got colder. Fear returned. She shivered. Goose bumps popped up on her arms. The chill ran up and down her back, into her spine. She reached up. Cold air entered the tunnel from a vent above her on the left wall. Only a vent. Not an exit.

She hurried on into warm, velvet blackness. Soon she wanted to stop, to curl up, to huddle as small as possible and hope he walked by. She was losing hope that she could get away from him. Sooner or later, she'd come to a dead end. Then he'd catch up to her. Finally she remembered. Mr. Sable. Where was he? Why wasn't he down here? Why didn't he help her?

Help me. Where are you? I need help. Please, oh, please come. Come and help me.

seventeen

———

"I'M HERE. AHEAD of you."

"Oh, thank God. I need help. Will you help me?"

"Of course I will. Come. Follow me."

She could not see him, but, as always, she sensed his presence. She followed, and with his lead, they moved quickly.

In no time at all they reached his studio, turning left off the tunnel. She smelled the paint, the turpentine, mixed with the dust. Now could she hide? Would her pursuer pass right by the doorway and lose her?

"Mr. Sable?" she whispered. He'd know what to do. "Mr. Sable!" He was gone. She was alone again. Why had he left her?

Without thinking, she swung around. Her hand slammed against an easel, knocking it sideways. Wooden boards crashed to the floor, causing what was probably a pile of paintings to slide and tumble down at the same time. She couldn't have made more noise if she had tried.

Despair gripped her. She tried to swallow her sobs as she slid down the wall behind her and crumpled to the floor.

"LaDonna?" He called her name. He knew her. The whisper, low and hoarse, sounded familiar, but she didn't recognize it. It did sound like the same whisper from the bridge, though. That night—the night Minette Waterson was killed. This was Minette's killer. Katherine's killer. Her killer.

She bit her lip, sucked in a scream, holding her breath.

"I know you're in here. Give up. I have you now."

His foot slid into her body, curled against the wall. Reaching down, he pulled her to her feet. His laughter was low, taunting.

"This place is even better than the music room. You can scream, shout all you like. No one will ever hear you, LaDonna."

"Stop it. Who are you? Leave me alone." LaDonna pounded her fists on his chest. She pulled and tugged to get away but his hands were like vice grips on her arms. All the while she struggled she kept thinking, who, who is this. His voice was almost level with her. Johnny was tall. His voice would come from higher up. Not Johnny—not Johnny—not Johnny. How could she have suspected him? Oh, thank God it wasn't Johnny.

She tried relaxing again. The move had worked before. He only tightened his hold on her.

"Such a talented artist," he whispered, spinning her around, catching both wrists in his one hand, long fingers biting into her flesh, keeping her prisoner.

Something cold pressed against her throat. She stopped struggling immediately, froze, her head held stiffly back. She didn't have to see the knife blade to know what was against her neck. One slash from him and she was dead, her life blood pooling on the floor of the studio like crimson oils in a swirl of anger and death.

"Why?" she whispered. Stall him. Get him to talk. "Why do you need to kill me? Who are you? Why do you hate me?"

"I don't hate you, LaDonna. You don't understand."

He was forgetting to whisper. His voice—that voice—it was—it was—

Suddenly, as if moon glow entered the windows, a dim light filled the studio.

Eric, the killer was Eric. Her stomach heaved. She groaned, squeezed her eyes closed, opened them again as if he would disappear. Be someone else. Someone she had never met. Someone she had never hated, then had started to know just today.

"Eric. You? How could you do this?"

His face twisted and he laughed at her. "How could I not? A student shouldn't have more talent than her teacher. Even her student teacher. Talent is given out so unfairly. Katherine had no time for me. She kept saying her music came first. And Minette, dear Minette. She hated me. Said I had no talent. You hated me at first, didn't you? And I was torn towards admiring you and hating you, LaDonna. Hate won. I'm sorry. I—I—"

Eric stared at something, someone behind her. The hatred that contorted his face changed, melted into intense fear.

"No, no. You—you can't—I—"

Before LaDonna could turn around, darkness filled the room again. She heard a soft thud, a groan from the man in front of her. She sensed, rather than saw, that he had fallen to the floor.

An image of the room burned in her mind. Before it could vanish, she stepped around the body on the floor and reached for the cord hanging from the light in the middle of the room.

When the light came on, she spun around to see who else was there. No one.

Grabbing a piece of rope that had held several canvases together, hoping it wasn't rotten with age, she rolled Eric onto his stomach, pulled his limp arms together, wrapped the rope around both of his hands. Knotting the soft rope securely around his hands, crying all the while, she found another piece and tied his ankles together.

She blanked her mind, tying the rope without thinking. She wanted the killer to be someone she didn't know. How could envy of someone's talent twist itself into such hatred, enough anger to kill? She drew deep breaths, stopped the hysteria starting to surface now that Eric was tied.

Eric groaned. Was he waking up? La-Donna knew she had to get help before he gained consciousness. She didn't want to deal with this any more by herself.

She turned and fled, savoring the warm darkness of the tunnel, feeling safe there. Hurrying, feeling *him* lead her towards greater safety.

eighteen

LaDonna slipped out of the art building, wondering where the nearest phone was. She was frantically trying to remember when someone called her name.

"LaDonna, ready to go home?" Johnny Blair bounced up to meet her. His dark frown was gone. Confessing he loved her had done wonders for his mood.

"Johnny, oh, Johnny." She fell into his arms.

"Hey, I thought we were going to stay cool. You missed me, huh?"

"Johnny. The man. I have the man. The murderer. Tied up in the basement."

Johnny stared at her, struck dumb by her announcement, certainly not what he expected her to say to him.

"A phone, I need a phone. I—I can't remember—"

He grabbed her hand and together they ran to the entrance of Old Main. LaDonna let Johnny dial 911 while she thought of what to say. "I have the campus killer," she blurted out.

Johnny grabbed the receiver. He was in control.

"We'll meet you in front of Old Main."

Everything that had happened hit LaDonna. She huddled in Johnny's arms, shivering, crying, while he dialed campus security.

"Oh, Johnny, it's Eric Hunter." LaDonna needed to talk before the police arrived.

"Eric? Are you sure? Why would Eric kill anyone?"

"I'm sure. He tried to kill me. He said he was envious of my—our talent. All those women's talents. Katherine. Minette. He knew them all."

"That doesn't seem like a good enough reason to kill." Johnny kept looking for the police. Two cars pulled up in front of Old Main and screeched to a halt.

"Are you the woman who called?" one officer asked LaDonna.

She nodded and motioned for them to follow her. Grabbing Johnny's hand, she ran.

Letting them into the art building with

her key, she led Johnny and four police-men into the bowels of the old building. Johnny paused for just seconds to look at her new painting, but she tugged on his hand.

"Do you have flashlights?" she asked the officers.

They nodded, took them out and flashed powerful beams into the tunnel behind the basement door. For the first time LaDonna saw the labyrinth she had traveled over and over. It amazed her that she had avoided all the wires, cables, and pipes.

I would have been more frightened if I could have seen this place, she thought, practically running now.

She had to concentrate to make the right turns. Any number of tunnels ran off the main one, leaving her in awe and fear at how lost she could have gotten had she not had help to come in here.

"How did you find this place?" asked Johnny, his voice filled with the same awe that LaDonna felt now that she could see the passageways.

"Never mind." Who was going to be-lieve her if she said she had help, a companion?

To her relief, Eric still lay on the floor in Mr. Sable's studio. He was conscious and had rubbed his wrists raw trying to escape before she returned.

Two policemen set him on his feet rather roughly. Eric stared at her. The hatred, the pure evil in his twisted face, in his eyes, caused her to take a step back from him. She bumped into Johnny, who circled her with both arms, pulling her shoulders to his chest.

"He attacked me as I left the campus tonight," LaDonna told her story. "I got away and he followed me here." She felt as if this Eric before her was someone she had never known.

"Why did you come in here?" one officer asked, his voice unbelieving. "How did you find your way?"

"I—I was desperate." She wasn't going to tell the truth—not yet anyway. "I knew the tunnels were underneath the campus. My—my father works in maintenance." There, that was a good explanation.

"Everyone knows there are tunnels under the campus," Johnny said, holding LaDonna tighter. Was he remembering the times she had confided in him, when she first met Mr. Sable and the other day?

"I've found an address here." One of the policemen had gone through Eric's pockets.

"He said he had an aunt living in Bellponte." LaDonna repeated what Eric had told her.

One of the policemen had been looking

at the paintings hung on the walls of the dusty studio room. He reached out.

"Don't touch them!" LaDonna surprised herself at the fierceness in her voice. "I—I mean, they need to be recovered, brought out of here and cleaned."

Eric had been watching, looking around himself. He seemed to have changed, his shoulders slumped, his face more like the sullen Eric she had seen many times. "I wondered where they were," he said, so quiet she might have been the only one who heard him.

"You know this artist?" LaDonna asked him.

He gave her a angry glance, then tightened his mouth as if to say, I never spoke.

"Officer Simms," LaDonna said, "are you going to check on that address tonight? Can I go with you to meet Eric's aunt?"

The policemen looked at each other. Simms made the decision. "I don't know how you got away from and caught this man, Miss Martindale, but we owe you. You can come."

LaDonna led the way back out of the tunnels to her basement. Then she stepped back and looked around the dark gallery where she had worked all spring. He was not here now. And somehow she knew he would never be back. She felt a terrible loss and pushed back the empty feeling around her heart. She hurried to follow the two policemen who walked on either side of Eric.

LaDonna grasped Johnny's hand and dared anyone to say he had to stay behind. They got into the back seat of the second patrol car. One car—the one with Eric in it—headed for the police station. Their car turned south, then west and finally pulled up in front of a tiny house on Bluebell Street. Another, unmarked car waited for them. The man who got out introduced himself as Detective McPhearson, in charge of the campus murder investigation.

To LaDonna's surprise, considering the time of night, one light burned in the front of the house.

"Mrs. Flores?" Officer Simms spoke through the small crack of open doorway. "I'm Officer Simms from the Bellponte Police. We need to ask you a couple of questions about someone we understand may be your nephew."

LaDonna, from behind the two officers, could hear Mrs. Flores sigh. "What has he done now? I told him to leave me alone."

"Could we come in?" Officer Simms asked.

Mrs. Flores reluctantly held open the door and stepped back. She seemed surprised to see LaDonna and Johnny follow the two police officers and the Detective who had met them at the Flores residence.

Detective McPhearson took over the inquiry. "Mrs. Flores, I understand you have a nephew named"—he looked at his notes—"Eric Hunter."

"He said he was my nephew." Mrs. Flores, a tiny woman with a neat bun at the back of her neck, must have been in her early eighties, but her brown eyes were sharp, her stance said, no foolishness, and the look on her face was one of resignation.

"Does anyone live here with you?" Detective McPhearson asked. Maybe he felt she might need some support on hearing about Eric's problems.

"I live alone by choice, Detective. Eric came to Bellponte last fall, claiming to be my nephew. He wanted to live here but I said no. He was rude and I didn't like him. One doesn't always have to like relatives, you know. I assume he is my sister's second daughter's child, and if so, he's been in trouble off and on all his life, so speak out. I won't be surprised at anything you have to tell me. Is he hurt?"

"No, it's not that. We're holding him as a suspect in the recent murders on campus. I'm sure you've read about them in the newspaper."

"I don't take a paper—nothing but bad news these days. Don't have TV either, young man. Television is for dimwits. Shame no one can see the potential there for educating these young people with too much time on their hands."

LaDonna liked this woman. Her heart went out to her, having to hear that any relative, even distant, had gone as bad as Eric. LaDonna glanced around the dim room they had entered.

She gasped.

Everyone looked at her. She jerked away from Johnny and ran to the far wall to look at the painting hanging there. Her hand moved to gently touch the picture.

"Don't touch that!" Mrs. Flores was beside her in a second.

"I—I'm sorry. I know this work, this artist, Mrs. Flores. I was startled to find one of his paintings here. Where did you get it?" LaDonna's eyes met those of Mrs. Flores. The tiny woman barely came to her shoulder, but she had a powerful aura that held LaDonna captive until she could look her over good.

Her face finally softened. "Do you like it?"

What to say? "I—I've been very influenced by this man's work. How do you know him?"

Mrs. Flores took LaDonna's hand and led her into the next room. Her fingers reached for the wall switch, throwing soft spots onto several paintings around the patio room.

"Ramon Flores was my husband, young woman." Mrs. Flores stopped in front of a portrait, surely her many years ago. She studied the picture while she spoke. "He had just started to attract the world's attention when he was fatally injured in a fire at the college sixty-five years ago. The world lost an incredible talent, and I lost a dear, gentle companion. I suspect that a great many paintings were also lost in the fire. I have not been able to share these few, and yet I know I must before I die. Eric Hunter had the nerve to ask me to leave them to him in my will. Today's young people think of nothing but money."

"Are they worth a lot of money?" Johnny had followed LaDonna.

"I suppose they are, but money means nothing to me at my age. Ramon and I were poor for so long, and then he decided to teach—I'm sure for my sake, since all he wanted to do was paint."

LaDonna found that she was speechless. She moved from painting to painting slowly, studying each.

Detective McPhearson had been patient as long as he could. "I must have a statement from you, Miss Martindale. I think we're finished here. But you'll need to come to the station with me and tell us what happened tonight. Would you like to call your parents?"

"Can Johnny go with me?" LaDonna looked at Johnny. She needed him more than she did her father.

He nodded. "I go with you or you don't go."

"And Detective McPhearson, I need a few more minutes with Mrs. Flores. Can't you go ahead and let Officer Simms give me a ride? I promise I won't be long."

Detective McPhearson looked impatient, but not unreasonable. "I guess so."

The police left together, talking, while LaDonna and Johnny stayed behind with Mrs. Flores.

LaDonna took the old woman's hand in hers. Her skin was so soft but her grip firm. LaDonna could feel a bond forming that hadn't been there before.

"Mrs. Flores, your husband's paintings weren't destroyed in the fire. I know where they are, and I'll see that you get them as soon as possible."

Mrs. Flores looked at LaDonna with disbelief. Before she could say anything, LaDonna continued. "And one more thing. I know the man who heads up the art gallery on campus. I'm working for him." And I've made a discovery greater than he would ever have expected, she added to herself. "I can't make any promises, but Mr. Flores's work does need to be shared with the public. If I can persuade Mr. Walker, I think a show is in order. And then perhaps a room in the gallery honoring your husband's work—named for him."

"I have been wondering what to do with my small estate, Miss Martindale." Mrs. Flores found her voice. "If what you tell me is really true, then I will endow this room for my husband's work." The tiny woman clasped her hands together, stared at one of her husband's paintings— one that reflected the joy that LaDonna was starting to feel—and smiled. LaDonna could see why early artists painted gold aura's above the head's of special women. It took little imagination to see this light around Mrs. Flores.

LaDonna knew she would never understand what had happened to her in her basement gallery. She could never explain how Mr. Flores had come to her and had worked with her. But right now, and maybe never, she didn't have to understand.

Nothing could balance out the deaths of three young, talented women on the campus, but LaDonna swore she was going to bring some beauty and art to the world to help compensate for the way life swings from darkness to light.

She had one more thing to say to Mrs. Flores before she faced the rest of this night. She put her arms around the woman, hoping it wasn't the wrong thing to do. When she stepped back, she saw an even stronger light around this beautiful woman.

Before LaDonna could say more, Mrs. Flores spoke. "I would like you to be my friend, LaDonna, if you are open to being friends with an old woman."

LaDonna knew she was only going to be able to say one more thing before she broke into tears. To say yes, we are already friends, she took both of Mrs. Flores's hands in her own.

"And I want you to know one more thing, Mrs. Flores." LaDonna swallowed the lump forming in her throat. "Your husband, Mr. Flores, was—is a very fine teacher."